MAKE WAY
FOR McCLOSKEY

MAKE WAY FOR McCLOSKEY

A Robert McCloskey Treasury

With an introduction by LEONARD S. MARCUS

VIKING

Photo credits: Page 1, from the Viking files; page 6, by Mary Velthoven; page 8 bottom, by Marc Simont; pages 9, 10 top and bottom, 142 top, back jacket, Suzanne Szasz/Photo Researchers, copyright © 1952; page 138, from the Viking files; page 139 top, courtesy the McCloskey family; bottom, by Djon Mili; page 141, top and bottom, from the Viking files; page 142 bottom, Minot, copyright © 1958; page 143 top and bottom, from the Viking files; page 144 bottom left, from the Viking files, bottom, by George Sagosch.

VIKING
Published by Penguin Group
Penguin Young Readers Group, 345 Hudson Street, New York, New York 10014, U.S.A.
Penguin Books Ltd, 80 Strand, London WC2R 0RL, England
Penguin Books Australia Ltd, 250 Camberwell Road, Camberwell, Victoria 3124, Australia
Penguin Books Canada Ltd, 10 Alcorn Avenue, Toronto, Ontario, Canada M4V 3B2
Penguin Group (NZ), cnr Airborne and Rosedale Roads, Albany, Auckland 1310, New Zealand

First published in 2004 by Viking, a division of Penguin Young Readers Group

20 19 18 17 16 15 14 13 12 11

LIBRARY OF CONGRESS CATALOGING-IN-PUBLICATION DATA
McCloskey, Robert, 1914–2003
Make way for McCloskey : a Robert McCloskey treasury / [by Robert McCloskey] ; introduction by Leonard S. Marcus.
v. cm.
Contents: Lentil—Make way for ducklings—Homer Price—Blueberries for Sal—Centerburg tales—One morning in Maine—Time of wonder—Burt Dow deep water man—About Robert McCloskey.
ISBN 978-0-670-05934-8 (hardcover)
1. Children's stories, American. [1. Short stories.] I. Marcus, Leonard S., 1950– II. Title.
PZ7.M47841419Mak 2004 [E]—dc22 2004004271

Manufactured in China
Set in New Caledonia
Book design by Edward Miller

CONTENTS

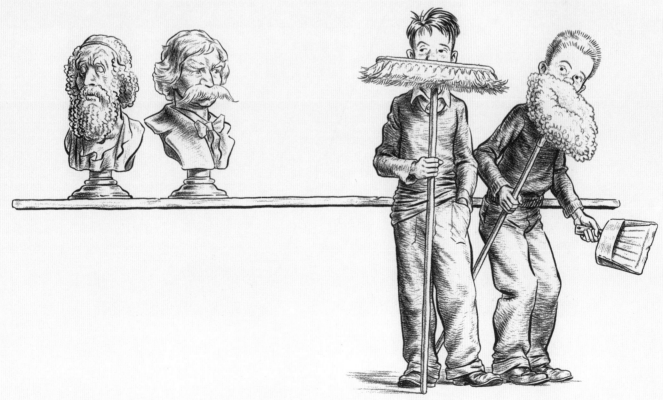

INTRODUCTION

Robert McCloskey (1914–2003) and the American picture book came of age together. "I didn't start life . . . with any burning desire to create little gems for the young," McCloskey told an audience in 1942 on accepting his first Caldecott Medal, for *Make Way for Ducklings*. No artist of his generation was likely to have said otherwise. Public library service to children—an inspired turn-of-the-last-century American invention—was then barely two generations old. Specialized publishing aimed at stocking the children's room shelves was newer still. Because most children's books required illustration, artists like McCloskey—those who did not look down their noses at the thought of creating artwork for "juveniles"—simply seized the moment by making the rounds of publishers' offices, portfolios in hand. McCloskey was thrilled when he realized he had chanced onto an art form that allowed him to build on his natural gifts as a storyteller, to experiment with composition and design, and to have his artwork *seen*. But he was not alone in expecting neither fame nor greater glory from an art still thought too lowly in the 1930s and 1940s to be taught at art schools or represented in the nation's museums.

Born in Hamilton, Ohio, and trained in Boston and New York, McCloskey pledged himself to a career in art during the first wave of American Scene Painting, a broadly based Depression-era movement that favored representation over abstraction and embraced everyday American life as worthy subject matter for art. As an unknown freelancer with the usual bills to pay, he tried his luck in every conceivable direction: drawing, printmaking, painting watercolors and murals. Illustration at first simply seemed one more potential outlet for his skills. During the second of his two exploratory visits to Viking Junior Books, the editor in charge, a fellow Midwesterner named May Massee, urged him to develop a picture book story he had sketched out based on life in his hometown. With the publication of *Lentil* in 1940, McCloskey

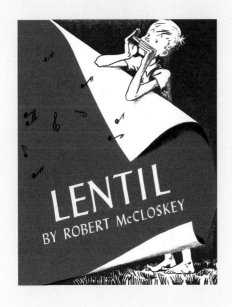

joined the illustrious roster of "Massee men" that by then included Robert Lawson, James Daugherty, Ludwig Bemelmans, Kurt Wiese, and William Pène du Bois. In one bold stroke, the earnest young Ohioan had found a mentor, a creative home, and a vocation.

A tall, shy, unpretentious man, McCloskey admired "know-how"—the word was a favorite of his—and abhorred all forms of self-importance and sham. A lifelong bad speller, he was a perfectionist in art, whose plain-spoken manner carried over into the unfussy line, solid conviction, and good-natured humor of his drawings. Despite the fame and fortune that did in fact come to him as his books earned medal after medal and reached a worldwide circle of readers, McCloskey, during an illustration career that spanned thirty years, always kept the artistic stakes for himself exceedingly high. He reminded an audience once that a picture book illustration "has to tell a lot of the story. Not 10,000 words of story, but a lot," and that a careless drawing might require "10,000 words to *explain*." Still grappling with the equation a half dozen years later, he said, "A picture is only worth as many ideas or words as someone puts into it with his pen or brush or snap of a shutter."

For most of his long public life, McCloskey regaled audiences with tales of the making of his second and best-loved book, *Make Way for Ducklings*: how, after months of observation in the Boston Public Garden and research at New York's American Museum of Natural History, he had felt the need to actually live with a family of ducklings in the Greenwich Village apartment he shared with fellow illustrator Marc Simont. How he had struggled to sketch the boisterous birds as they splashed in the tub and skittered from room to room of the apartment. How he had finally had to find some way to slow them down. "The only thing that worked," he said, as though reporting matter-of-factly on the weather, "was red wine. They loved it and went into slow motion right away."

McCloskey became an illustrator at a time when publishers still regarded full-color printing as a major financial risk. As he started work on *Make Way for Ducklings*, he tried but failed to persuade Massee of his ability to control color, and was told to do his best with line. Choosing sepia rather than

Drawing of McCloskey by Marc Simont, 1938.

standard black for both the type and drawings, because of the feeling of warmth it contributed, McCloskey proceeded to push the picture book format to the limit. He aimed, he later said, to infuse his panoramic lithographic drawings with the "feel" of color, to cram the bigness of a mural into each of the book's open spreads, to show Boston from a "duck's-eye view." Detail was selective, edited from a child's, as well as a duck's, perspective. "No one," he decided, was "going to go strolling or flying over and check the number of chimneys that I put on or the number of bricks. But the detail of a wrought-iron fence . . . that a child would put his hand on or walk right by or rub a stick on the way children do—that's accurate." Not everyone had yet heard of the Caldecott Medal when in 1942 McCloskey became its fifth recipient. He later claimed to have still been among those in the dark right up until the moment he received the good news.

Before reporting for World War II military service the following year, McCloskey finished the first of his two longer storybooks, *Homer Price*. In Homer—a youngster brimming with decency, stick-to-itiveness, and good sense—McCloskey captured the essence of the all-American boy. Just as the departing Mr.

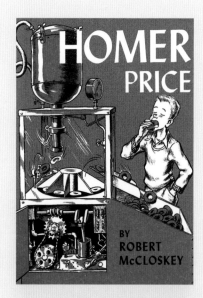

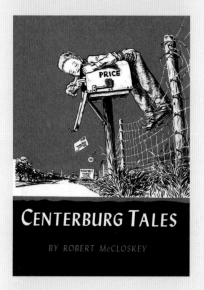

Working in his studio, 1952.

On his boat with his daughters and
pet English setter, Penny, 1952.

McCloskey and his daughters Sally and
Jane in 1952 in Mr. Condon's store, which
is depicted in *One Morning in Maine*.

Mallard's promise of a swift and safe return gained new meaning in wartime, Homer too struck a chord in readers anxious for reminders of the values that they as Americans cherished.

It was after the war that McCloskey discovered Maine. He was married by then and had become a father. Starting with *Blueberries for Sal*, his picture books take on the casual, unguarded feeling of home movies. With a seemingly unself-conscious ease that distilled Americans' longing for peace and perspective in still-turbulent times, McCloskey turned to himself, his wife, and their two young daughters as subjects to draw, and to the Maine island home where they spent half the year as the setting for stories of close-knit family life framed by the larger rhythms of nature. The baby boom had greatly expanded the market for children's books, with those bearing Caldecott Medals topping many peoples' shopping lists. By the time *Blueberries for Sal* came along in the fall of 1948, a new McCloskey book had the aura of a national event. That December, *Life* magazine reprinted the story in its entirety as "a Christmas gift to our younger readers."

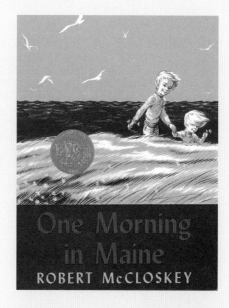

In *One Morning in Maine* and *Time of Wonder* (his second Caldecott–Medal winner) McCloskey offered readers further glimpses of family and island life from a lightly held but ever-deepening spiritual perspective. By then it had long since become clear that along with Frank Capra, Norman Rockwell, and Irving Berlin, McCloskey was one of the dream-catchers of his generation, a popular artist able, through a combination of lyricism, humor, compassion, and story, to limn the universal dimension in the everyday. Little Sal coping with a lost tooth is *every* child making her way, one small but stupendous step at a time, up the ladder of self-discovery. The Boston of *Make Way for Ducklings* is a modern-day peaceable kingdom: the city and nature harmonized, the perfect place to raise the kids.

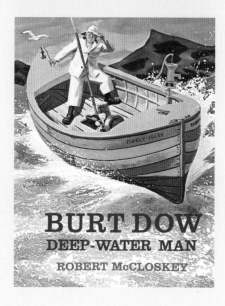

But not everything in McCloskey's books is ideal. The *Homer Price* story about the "unpredictable automatic dough-nut machine" raises the specter of modern technology gone haywire. In the pivotal scene of *Burt Dow, Deep-Water Man*, McCloskey shows modern art perhaps taking a comparable turn. Trapped Jonah-like inside the belly of a whale, Burt hurls whole canloads of grease and paint at the sea creature's inner stomach wall, hoping to sicken the whale just enough to make

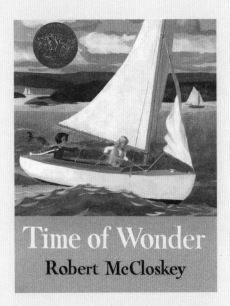

Time of Wonder
Robert McCloskey

it spit the fisherman up to safety. Burt's splatterings, which bear a more than passing resemblance to a Jackson Pollock, do the trick all right. With sly understatement, McCloskey leaves readers to sort out the elusive connections between nausea, Abstract Expressionism, and a good life spared.

Whatever else McCloskey may have thought of modern painting, he was fascinated by the paradox that art, however realistic, is always an abstraction, a drawing-board construct made valid not only by the artist's skill but by the quality of his intention. It amused him to have created the quintessential picture book about Boston while in a Greenwich Village studio awash with Long Island ducklings; to have based his illustration of Homer Price, the archetypal small-town American boy, on sketches of a gangly young New Yorker; to have drawn the bears needed for *Blueberries for Sal* at the Central Park Zoo. Incongruities such as these were, however, simply artist's tricks of the trade and of no great importance when placed beside the deceptive practices of old-fashioned flimflam artists like the one McCloskey satirized in the "Ever So Much More So" adventure of *Centerburg Tales*, or their modern counterparts in television commercials.

In his second Caldecott acceptance speech, given months after the Soviet launch of *Sputnik I* and *II*, and against the backdrop of frantic American calls for more and better and faster science education, McCloskey offered a contrarian view. What Americans really needed just then, he said, was to learn how to *see*, how to tell for themselves the difference between a deceptive advertising image and an honestly informative one, between a well-designed house or city or world and one that threatened to upend the balance of nature. There was no better way, McCloskey argued, for children or anyone to acquire and master that essential skill than by learning how to draw.

Half a century later, art education too often remains a frill at school rather than the vital life lesson he believed it could be. But Robert McCloskey's own evergreen stories and pictures still inspire us to look closer at things: at the beauty of nature, the strength of family, the meaning of home—at what really matters in life and why.

—Leonard S. Marcus
March 2004

MAKE WAY
FOR
DUCKLINGS

1941

Mr. and Mrs. Mallard were looking for a place to live. But every time Mr. Mallard saw what looked like a nice place, Mrs. Mallard said it was no good. There were sure to be foxes in the woods or turtles in the water, and she was not going to raise a family where there might be foxes or turtles. So they flew on and on.

When they got to Boston, they felt too tired to fly any further. There was a nice pond in the Public Garden, with a little island on it. "The very place to spend the night," quacked Mr. Mallard. So down they flapped.

Next morning they fished for their
breakfast in the mud at the bottom of
the pond. But they didn't find much.

Just as they were getting ready to start on their way, a strange enormous bird came
by. It was pushing a boat full of people, and there was a man sitting on its back. "Good
morning," quacked Mr. Mallard, being polite. The big bird was
too proud to answer. But the people on the boat threw peanuts
into the water, so the Mallards followed them all round the
pond and got another breakfast, better than the first.

"I like this place," said Mrs. Mallard as they climbed out on the bank and waddled along. "Why don't we build a nest and raise our ducklings right in this pond? There are no foxes and no turtles, and the people feed us peanuts. What could be better?"

"Good," said Mr. Mallard, delighted that at last Mrs. Mallard had found a place that suited her. But—

"Look out!" squawked Mrs. Mallard, all of a dither. "You'll get run over!" And when she got her breath she added: "*This* is no place for babies, with all those horrid things rushing about. We'll have to look somewhere else."

So they flew over Beacon Hill and round the State House, but there was no place there.

They looked in Louisburg Square, but there was no water to swim in.

Then they flew over the Charles River. "This is better," quacked Mr. Mallard. "That island looks like a nice quiet place, and it's only a little way from the Public Garden."

"Yes," said Mrs. Mallard, remembering the peanuts. "That looks like just the right place to hatch ducklings."

So they chose a cozy spot among the bushes near the water and settled down to build their nest. And only just in time, for now they were beginning to molt. All their old wing feathers started to drop out, and they would not be able to fly again until the new ones grew in.

But of course they could swim, and one day they swam over to the park on the river bank, and there they met a policeman called Michael. Michael fed them peanuts, and after that the Mallards called on Michael every day.

After Mrs. Mallard had laid eight eggs in the nest she couldn't go to visit Michael any more, because she had to sit on the eggs to keep them warm. She moved off the nest only to get a drink of water, or to have her lunch, or to count the eggs and make sure they were all there.

One day the ducklings hatched out. First came Jack, then Kack, and then Lack, then Mack and Nack and Ouack and Pack and Quack. Mr. and Mrs. Mallard were bursting with pride. It was a great responsibility taking care of so many ducklings, and it kept them very busy.

One day Mr. Mallard decided he'd like to take a trip to see what the rest of the river was like, further on. So off he set. "I'll meet you in a week, in the Public Garden," he quacked over his shoulder. "Take good care of the ducklings."

"Don't you worry," said Mrs. Mallard. "I know all about bringing up children." And she did.

She taught them how to swim and dive.

She taught them to walk in a line, to come when they were called, and to keep a safe distance from bikes and scooters and other things with wheels.

When at last she felt perfectly satisfied with them, she said one morning: "Come along, children. Follow me."

Before you could wink an eyelash Jack, Kack, Lack, Mack, Nack, Ouack, Pack, and Quack fell into line, just as they had been taught. Mrs. Mallard led the way into the water and they swam behind her to the opposite bank.

There they waded ashore and waddled along till they came to the highway.

Mrs. Mallard stepped out to cross the road. "Honk, honk!" went the horns on the speeding cars. "Qua-a-ack!" went Mrs. Mallard as she tumbled back again. "Quack! Quack! Quack! Quack!" went Jack, Kack, Lack, Mack, Nack, Ouack, Pack, and Quack, just as loud as their little quackers could quack. The cars kept speeding by and honking, and Mrs. Mallard and the ducklings kept right on quack-quack-quacking.

They made such a noise that Michael came running, waving his arms and blowing his whistle.

He planted himself in the center
of the road, raised one hand to stop
the traffic, and then beckoned with
the other, the way policemen do, for
Mrs. Mallard to cross over.

As soon as Mrs. Mallard and the ducklings
were safe on the other side and on their way
down Mount Vernon Street, Michael rushed
back to his police booth.

He called Clancy at headquarters and
said: "There's a family of ducks walkin'
down the street!" Clancy said: "Family of
what?" *"Ducks!"* yelled Michael. "Send
a police car, quick!"

Meanwhile, Mrs. Mallard had reached the Corner Book Shop and turned into
Charles Street, with Jack, Kack, Lack,
Mack, Nack, Ouack, Pack, and Quack
all marching in line behind her.

Everyone stared. An old lady from Beacon Hill said: "Isn't it amazing!" and the man who swept the streets said: "Well, now, ain't that nice!" and when Mrs. Mallard heard them she was so proud she tipped her nose in the air and walked along with an extra swing in her waddle.

When they came to the corner of Beacon Street there was the police car with four policemen that Clancy had sent from headquarters. The policemen held back the traffic so Mrs. Mallard and the ducklings could march across the street,

right on into the Public Garden.

Inside the gate they all turned around to say thank you to the policemen. The policemen smiled and waved good-by.

When they reached the pond and swam across to the little island, there was Mr. Mallard waiting for them, just as he had promised.

The ducklings liked the new island so much that they decided to live there. All day long they follow the swan boats and eat peanuts.

And when night falls they swim to their little island and go to sleep.

BLUEBERRIES
FOR SAL

1948

One day, Little Sal went with her mother to
Blueberry Hill to pick blueberries.

Little Sal brought along her small tin pail and her
mother brought her large tin pail to put berries in. "We
will take our berries home and can them," said her
mother. "Then we will have food for the winter."

Little Sal picked three berries and
dropped them in her little tin pail . . .
kuplink, kuplank, kuplunk!

She picked three more berries and ate
them. Then she picked more berries and
dropped one in the pail—*kuplunk!* And
the rest she ate. Then Little Sal ate all
four blueberries out of her pail!

Her mother walked slowly through the bushes, picking blueberries as she went and putting them in her pail. Little Sal struggled along behind, picking blueberries and eating every single one.

Little Sal hurried ahead and dropped a blueberry in her mother's pail. It didn't sound *kuplink!* because the bottom of the pail was already covered with berries. She reached down inside to get her berry back. Though she really didn't mean to, she pulled out a large handful, because there were so many blueberries right up close to the one she had put in.

Her mother stopped picking and said, "Now, Sal, you run along and pick your own berries. Mother wants to take her berries home and can them for next winter."

Her mother went back to her picking, but Little Sal, because her feet were tired of standing and walking, sat down in the middle of a large clump of bushes and ate blueberries.

On the other side of Blueberry Hill, Little Bear came with his mother to eat blueberries.

"Little Bear," she said, "eat lots of berries and grow big and fat. We must store up food for the long, cold winter."

Little Bear followed behind his mother as she walked slowly through the bushes eating berries. Little Bear stopped now and then to eat berries.

Then he had to hustle along to catch up!

Because his feet were tired of hustling, he picked out a large clump of bushes and sat down right in the middle and ate blueberries.

Over on the other side of the hill, Little Sal ate all of the berries she could reach from where she was sitting, then she started out to find her mother.

She heard a noise from around a rock and thought,
"That is my mother walking along!"

But it was a mother crow and her
children, and they stopped eating berries
and flew away, saying, "Caw, Caw, Caw."
Then she heard another noise in the
bushes and thought, "That is *surely* my
mother and I will go that way."

But it was Little Bear's mother instead. She was tramping along, eating berries, and thinking about storing up food for the winter. Little Sal tramped right along behind.

By this time, Little Bear had eaten all the berries he could reach without moving from his clump of bushes. Then he hustled off to catch up with his mother. He hunted and hunted but his mother was nowhere to be seen. He heard a noise from over a stump and thought, "That is my mother walking along."

But it was a mother partridge and her children. They stopped eating berries and hurried away. Then he heard a noise in the bushes and thought, "That is surely *my* mother. I will hustle that way!"

But it was Little Sal's mother instead! She was walking along, picking berries, and thinking about canning them for next winter. Little Bear hustled right along behind.

Little Bear and Little Sal's mother and Little Sal and
Little Bear's mother were all mixed up with each other
among the blueberries on Blueberry Hill.

Little Bear's mother heard Sal walking along behind and thought it was Little Bear
and she said, "Little Bear," *munch, munch*, "Eat all you—" *gulp*, "can possibly hold!"
swallow. Little Sal said nothing. She picked three berries and dropped them, *kuplink*,
kuplank, *kuplunk*, in her small tin pail.

Little Bear's mother turned around to see what on earth could make a noise like *kuplunk!*

"*Garumpf!*" she cried, choking on a mouthful of berries, "This is not my child! Where is Little Bear?" She took one good look and backed away. (She was old enough to be shy of people, even a very small person like Little Sal.) Then she turned around and walked off very fast to hunt for Little Bear.

Little Sal's mother heard Little Bear tramping along behind and thought it was Little Sal. She kept right on picking and thinking about canning blueberries for next winter.

Little Bear padded up and peeked into her pail. Of course, he only wanted to taste a *few* of what was inside, but there were so many and they were so close together, that he tasted a Tremendous Mouthful by mistake. "Now, Sal," said Little Sal's mother without turning around, "you run along and pick your own berries. Mother wants to can these for next winter." Little Bear tasted another Tremendous Mouthful, and almost spilled the entire pail of blueberries!

Little Sal's mother turned around and gasped, "My Goodness, *you* are not Little Sal! Where, oh where, is my child?"

Little Bear just sat munching and munching and swallowing and licking his lips.

Little Sal's mother slowly backed away. (She was old enough to be shy of bears, even very small bears like Little Bear.) Then she turned and walked away quickly to look for Little Sal.

She hadn't gone very far before she heard a
kuplink! kuplank! kuplunk!
She knew just what made that kind of a noise!

Little Bear's mother had not hunted very
long before she heard a hustling sound that
stopped now and then to munch and swallow.
She knew just what made that kind of a noise.

Little Bear and his mother went home down one side of Blueberry Hill, eating blueberries all the way, and full of food stored up for next winter.

And Little Sal and her mother went down the other side of Blueberry Hill, picking berries all the way, and drove home with food to can for next winter—a whole pail of blueberries and three more besides.

The Doughnuts

from

HOMER PRICE

1943

One Friday night in November Homer overheard his mother talking on the telephone to Aunt Agnes over in Centerburg. "I'll stop by with the car in about half an hour and we can go to the meeting together," she said, because tonight was the night the Ladies' Club was meeting to discuss plans for a box social and to knit and sew for the Red Cross.

"I think I'll come along and keep Uncle Ulysses company while you and Aunt Agnes are at the meeting," said Homer.

So after Homer had combed his hair and his mother had looked to see if she had her knitting instructions and the right size needles, they started for town.

Homer's Uncle Ulysses and Aunt Agnes have a very up and coming lunch room over in Centerburg, just across from the court house on the town square. Uncle Ulysses is a man with advanced ideas and a weakness for labor saving devices. He equipped the lunch room with automatic toasters, automatic coffee maker, automatic dish washer, and an automatic doughnut maker. All just the latest thing in labor saving devices. Aunt Agnes would throw up her hands and sigh every time Uncle Ulysses bought a new labor saving device. Sometimes she became unkindly disposed toward him for days and days. She was of the opinion that Uncle Ulysses just frittered away his spare time over at the barber shop with the sheriff and the boys, so, what was the good of a labor saving device that gave you more time to fritter?

When Homer and his mother got to Centerburg they stopped at the lunch room, and after Aunt Agnes had come out and said, "My, how that boy does grow!" which was what she always said, she went off with Homer's mother in the car. Homer went into the lunch room and said, "Howdy, Uncle Ulysses!"

"Oh, hello, Homer. You're just in time," said Uncle Ulysses. "I've been going over this automatic doughnut machine, oiling the machinery and cleaning the works . . . wonderful things, these labor saving devices."

"Yep," agreed Homer, and he picked up a cloth and started polishing the metal trimmings while Uncle Ulysses tinkered with the inside workings.

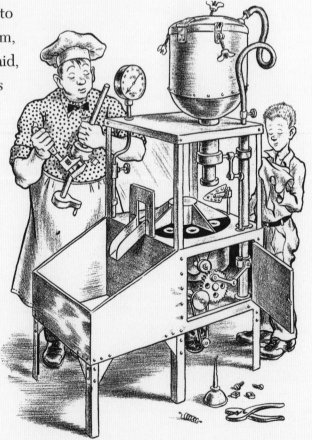

"Opfwo-oof!!" sighed Uncle Ulysses and, "Look here, Homer, you've got a mechanical mind. See if you can find where these two pieces fit in. I'm going across to the barber shop for a spell, 'cause there's somethin' I've got to talk to the sheriff about. There won't be much business here until the double feature is over and I'll be back before then."

Then as Uncle Ulysses went out the door he said, "Uh, Homer, after you get the pieces in place, would you mind mixing up a batch of doughnut batter and putting it in the machine? You could turn the switch and make a few doughnuts to have on hand for the crowd after the movie . . . if you don't mind."

"O.K." said Homer, "I'll take care of everything."

A few minutes later a customer came in and said, "Good evening, Bud."

Homer looked up from putting the last piece in the doughnut machine and said, "Good evening, Sir, what can I do for you?"

"Well, young feller, I'd like a cup o' coffee and some doughnuts," said the customer.

"I'm sorry, Mister, but we won't have any doughnuts for about half an hour, until I can mix some dough and start this machine. I could give you some very fine sugar rolls instead."

"Well, Bud, I'm in no real hurry so I'll just have a cup o' coffee and wait around a bit for the doughnuts. Fresh doughnuts are always worth waiting for is what I always say."

"O.K.," said Homer, and he drew a cup of coffee from Uncle Ulysses' super automatic coffee maker.

"Nice place you've got here," said the customer.

"Oh, yes," replied Homer, "this is a very up and coming lunch room with all the latest improvements."

"Yes," said the stranger, "must be a good business. I'm in business too. A traveling man in outdoor advertising. I'm a sandwich man, Mr. Gabby's my name."

"My name is Homer. I'm glad to meet you, Mr. Gabby. It must be a fine profession, traveling and advertising sandwiches."

"Oh no," said Mr. Gabby, "I don't advertise sandwiches, I just wear any kind of an ad, one sign on front and one sign on behind, this way . . . Like a sandwich. Ya know what I mean?"

"Oh, I see. That must be fun, and you travel too?" asked Homer as he got out the flour and the baking powder.

"Yeah, I ride the rods between jobs, on freight trains, ya know what I mean?"

"Yes, but isn't that dangerous?" asked Homer.

"Of course there's a certain amount a risk, but you take any method of travel these days, it's all dangerous. Ya know what I mean? Now take airplanes for instance . . . "

Just then a large shiny black car stopped in front of the lunch room and a chauffeur helped a lady out of the rear door. They both came inside and the lady smiled at Homer and said, "We've stopped for a light snack. Some doughnuts and coffee would be simply marvelous."

Then Homer said, "I'm sorry, Ma'm, but the doughnuts won't be ready until I make this batter and start Uncle Ulysses' doughnut machine."

"Well now aren't *you* a clever young man to know how to make *doughnuts!*"

"Well," blushed Homer, "I've really never done it before but I've got a receipt to follow."

"Now, young man, you simply must allow me to help. You know, I haven't made doughnuts for years, but I know the best receipt for doughnuts. It's marvelous, and we really must use it."

"But, Ma'm . . . " said Homer.

"Now just *wait* till you taste these doughnuts," said the lady. "Do you have an apron?" she asked, as she took off her fur coat and her rings and her jewelry and rolled up her sleeves. "Charles," she said to the chauffeur, "hand me that baking powder, that's right, and, young man, we'll need some nutmeg."

So Homer and the chauffeur stood by and handed things and cracked the eggs while the lady mixed and stirred. Mr. Gabby sat on his stool, sipped his coffee, and looked on with great interest.

"There!" said the lady when all of the ingredients were mixed. "Just *wait* till you taste these doughnuts!"

"It looks like an awful lot of batter," said Homer as he stood on a chair and poured it into the doughnut machine with the help of the chauffeur. "It's about *ten* times as much as Uncle Ulysses ever makes."

"But wait till you taste them!" said the lady with an eager look and a smile.

Homer got down from the chair and pushed a button on the machine marked, "*Start.*" Rings of batter started dropping into the hot fat. After a ring of batter was cooked on one side an automatic gadget turned it over and the other side would cook. Then another automatic gadget gave the doughnut a little push and it rolled neatly down a little chute, all ready to eat.

"That's a simply *fascinating* machine," said the lady as she waited for the first doughnut to roll out.

"Here, young man, *you* must have the first one. Now isn't that just *too* delicious? Isn't it simply marvelous?"

"Yes, Ma'm, it's very good," replied Homer as the lady handed doughnuts to Charles and to Mr. Gabby and asked if they didn't think they were simply divine doughnuts.

"It's an old family receipt!" said the lady with pride.

Homer poured some coffee for the lady and her chauffeur and for Mr. Gabby, and a glass of milk for himself. Then they all sat down at the lunch counter to enjoy another few doughnuts apiece.

"I'm so glad you enjoy my doughnuts," said the lady. "But now, Charles, we really must be going. If you will just take this apron, Homer, and put two dozen doughnuts in a bag to take along, we'll be on our way. And, Charles, don't forget to pay the young man." She rolled down her sleeves and put on her jewelry, then Charles managed to get her into her big fur coat.

"Good night, young man, I haven't had so much fun in years. I *really* haven't!" said the lady, as she went out the door and into the big shiny car.

"Those are sure good doughnuts," said Mr. Gabby as the car moved off.

"You bet!" said Homer. Then he and Mr. Gabby stood and watched the automatic doughnut machine make doughnuts.

After a few dozen more doughnuts had rolled down the little chute, Homer said, "I guess that's about enough doughnuts to sell to the after theater customers. I'd better turn the machine off for a while."

Homer pushed the button marked "*Stop*" and there was a little click, but nothing happened. The rings of batter kept right on dropping into the hot fat, and an automatic gadget kept right on turning them over, and another automatic gadget kept right on giving them a little push and the doughnuts kept right on rolling down the little chute, all ready to eat.

"That's funny," said Homer, "I'm sure that's the right button!" He pushed it again but the automatic doughnut maker kept right on making doughnuts.

"Well I guess I must have put one of those pieces in backwards," said Homer.

"Then it might stop if you pushed the button marked "*Start*," said Mr. Gabby.

Homer did, and the doughnuts still kept rolling down the little chute, just as regular as a clock can tick.

"I guess we could sell a few more doughnuts," said Homer, "but I'd better telephone Uncle Ulysses over at the barber shop." Homer gave the number and while he waited for someone to answer he counted thirty-seven doughnuts roll down the little chute.

Finally someone answered "Hello! This is the sarber bhop, I mean the barber shop."

"Oh, hello, sheriff. This is Homer. Could I speak to Uncle Ulysses?"

"Well, he's playing pinochle right now," said the sheriff. "Anythin' I can tell 'im?"

"Yes," said Homer. "I pushed the button marked *Stop* on the doughnut machine but the rings of batter keep right on dropping into the hot fat, and an automatic gadget keeps right on turning them over, and another automatic gadget keeps giving them a little push, and the doughnuts keep right on rolling down the little chute! It won't stop!"

"O.K. Wold the hire, I mean, hold the wire and I'll tell 'im." Then Homer looked over his shoulder and counted another twenty-one doughnuts roll down the little chute, all ready to eat. Then the sheriff said, "He'll be right over. . . . Just gotta finish this hand."

"That's good," said Homer. "G'by, sheriff."

The window was full of doughnuts by now so Homer and Mr. Gabby had to hustle around and start stacking them on plates and trays and lining them up on the counter.

"Sure are a lot of doughnuts!" said Homer.

"You bet!" said Mr. Gabby. "I lost count at twelve hundred and two and that was quite a while back."

People had begun to gather outside the lunch room window, and someone was saying, "There are almost as many doughnuts as there are people in Centerburg, and I wonder how in tarnation Ulysses thinks he can sell all of 'em!"

Every once in a while somebody would come inside and buy some, but while somebody bought two to eat and a dozen to take home, the machine made three dozen more.

By the time Uncle Ulysses and the sheriff arrived and pushed through the crowd, the lunch room was a calamity of doughnuts! Doughnuts in the window, doughnuts piled high on the shelves, doughnuts stacked on plates, doughnuts lined up twelve deep all along the counter, and doughnuts still rolling down the little chute, just as regular as a clock can tick.

"Hello, sheriff, hello, Uncle Ulysses, we're having a little trouble here," said Homer.

"Well, I'll be dunked!!" said Uncle Ulysses.

"Dernd ef you won't be when Aggy gits home," said the sheriff.

"Mighty fine doughnuts though. What'll you do with 'em all, Ulysses?"

Uncle Ulysses groaned and said, "What will Aggy say? We'll never sell 'em all."

Then Mr. Gabby, who hadn't said anything for a long time, stopped piling doughnuts and said, "What you need is an advertising man. Ya know what I mean? You got the doughnuts, ya gotta create a market . . . Understand? . . . It's balancing the demand with the supply . . . That sort of thing."

"Yep!" said Homer. "Mr. Gabby's right. We have to enlarge our market. He's an advertising sandwich man, so if we hire him, he can walk up and down in front of the theater and get the customers."

"You're hired, Mr. Gabby!" said Uncle Ulysses.

Then everybody pitched in to paint the signs and to get Mr. Gabby sandwiched between. They painted "SALE ON DOUGHNUTS" in big letters on the window too.

Meanwhile the rings of batter kept right on dropping into the hot fat, and an automatic gadget kept right on turning them over, and another automatic gadget kept right on giving them a little push, and the doughnuts kept right on rolling down the little chute, just as regular as a clock can tick.

"I certainly hope this advertising works," said Uncle Ulysses, wagging his head. "Aggy'll certainly throw a fit if it don't."

The sheriff went outside to keep order, because there was quite a crowd by now—all looking at the doughnuts and guessing how many thousands there were, and watching new ones roll down the little chute, just as regular as a clock can tick. Homer and Uncle Ulysses kept stacking doughnuts. Once in a while somebody bought a few, but not very often.

Then Mr. Gabby came back and said, "Say, you know there's not much use o' me advertisin' at the theater. The show's all over, and besides almost everybody in town is out front watching that machine make doughnuts!"

"Zeus!" said Uncle Ulysses. "We must get rid of these doughnuts before Aggy gets here!"

"Looks like you will have ta hire a truck ta waul 'em ahay, I mean haul 'em away!!" said the sheriff who had just come in. Just then there was a noise and a shoving out front and the lady from the shiny black car and her chauffeur came pushing through the crowd and into the lunch room.

"Oh, gracious!" she gasped, ignoring the doughnuts, "I've lost my diamond bracelet, and I know I left it here on the counter," she said, pointing to a place where the doughnuts were piled in stacks of two dozen.

"Yes, Ma'm, I guess you forgot it when you helped make the batter," said Homer.

Then they moved all the doughnuts around and looked for the diamond bracelet, but they couldn't find it anywhere. Meanwhile the doughnuts kept rolling down the little chute, just as regular as a clock can tick.

After they had looked all around the sheriff cast a suspicious eye on Mr. Gabby, but Homer said, "He's all right, sheriff, he didn't take it. He's a friend of mine."

Then the lady said, "I'll offer a reward of one hundred dollars for that bracelet! It really *must* be found! . . . it *really* must!"

"Now don't you worry, lady," said the sheriff. "I'll get your bracelet back!"

"Zeus! This is terrible!" said Uncle Ulysses. "First all of these doughnuts and then on top of all that, a lost diamond bracelet . . ."

Mr. Gabby tried to comfort him, and he said, "There's always a bright side. That machine'll probably run outta batter in an hour or two."

If Mr. Gabby hadn't been quick on his feet Uncle Ulysses would have knocked him down, sure as fate.

Then while the lady wrung her hands and said, "We must find it, we *must!*" and Uncle Ulysses was moaning about what Aunt Agnes would say, and the sheriff was eyeing Mr. Gabby, Homer sat down and thought hard.

Before twenty more doughnuts could roll down the little chute he shouted, "SAY! I know where the bracelet is! It was lying here on the counter and got mixed up in the batter by mistake! The bracelet is cooked inside one of these doughnuts!"

"Why . . . I really believe you're right," said the lady through her tears. "Isn't that *amazing?* Simply *amazing!*"

"I'll be durn'd!" said the sheriff.

"OhH-h!" moaned Uncle Ulysses. "Now we have to break up all of these doughnuts to find it. Think of the *pieces!* Think of the *crumbs!* Think of what *Aggy* will say!"

"Nope," said Homer. "We won't have to break them up. I've got a plan."

So Homer and the advertising man took some cardboard and some paint and printed another sign. They put this sign in the window, and the sandwich man wore two more signs that said the same thing and walked around in the crowd out front.

FRESH DOUGHNUTS
2 FOR 5¢
$ WHILE THEY LAST
100.⁰⁰ PRIZE
FOR FINDING
A BRACELET
INSIDE A DOUGHNUT
P.S. YOU HAVE TO GIVE THE
BRACELET BACK

THEN . . . The doughnuts began to sell! *Everybody* wanted to buy doughnuts, *dozens* of doughnuts!

And that's not all. Everybody bought coffee to dunk the doughnuts in too. Those that didn't buy coffee bought milk or soda. It kept Homer and the lady and the chauffeur and Uncle Ulysses and the sheriff busy waiting on the people who wanted to buy doughnuts.

When all but the last couple of hundred doughnuts had been sold, Rupert Black shouted, "I GAWT IT!" and sure enough . . . there was the diamond bracelet inside of his doughnut!

Then Rupert went home with a hundred dollars, the citizens of Centerburg went home full of doughnuts, the lady and her chauffeur drove off with the diamond bracelet, and Homer went home with his mother when she stopped by with Aunt Aggy.

As Homer went out of the door he heard Mr. Gabby say, "Neatest trick of merchandising I ever seen," and Aunt Aggy was looking skeptical while Uncle Ulysses was saying, "The rings of batter kept right on dropping into the hot fat, and the automatic gadget kept right on turning them over, and the other automatic gadget kept right on giving them a little push, and the doughnuts kept right on rolling down the little chute just as regular as a clock can tick—they just kept right on a comin', an' a comin', an' a comin', an' a comin'."

BURT DOW
DEEP-WATER MAN

A Tale of the Sea in the Classic Tradition

1963

Burt Dow is an old deep-water man, retired of course, but retired or not he still keeps two boats. One is a dory so old and so leaky that it can no longer be launched. Burt has painted it red and placed it on the little patch of lawn in front of his house, overlooking the bay.

He's rigged it like one of the many ships he's sailed to all the corners of all the seven seas. It's filled plumb to the gun'ls with earth, and every summer Burt plants it with geraniums and Indian peas. The geraniums brighten up the deck, and the Indian peas climb the rigging and sway this-a-way, that-a-way, in a smoky sou'wester.

The other boat is an old double-ender named *Tidely-Idley*, with a make-and-break engine. This boat leaks too, except when it's pulled up on shore for caulking, patching, and painting, which is most of the time.

"She's a good boat," says Burt, patting her on the stern and giving her propeller an affectionate kick. "She's got a few tender places in her planking, but you can't see daylight through her nowheres."

The *Tidely-Idley* is the pride and joy of Burt's life, and between odd jobs for natives and summer people he keeps her painted and patched as best he can. Every time he does a paint job, he brings home the leftover paint and uses it on the *Tidely-Idley*.

"That pink plank," he says, "is the color of Ginny Poor's pantry . . . and the green one is the color of the floor and doors in Doc Walton's waiting-room . . . and there's the tan porch and trim color from Capt'n Haskell's house."

Burt Dow has a sister named Leela who keeps house for him, cooks the lobsters and fish he catches and the clams he digs. She feeds the cock, she feeds the hens, she tends the garden, and she helps Burt keep down the weeds in the dory full of geraniums and Indian peas.

Leela is a very impatient person—"Most impatient being on land or sea," says Burt, and he hustles about doing this or that so as not to keep her waiting.

Mornings, when the cock crows, "Cockety-doodly," Leela is already down in the kitchen rattling her stove lids, klinkety-klink, and shouting, "Hit the deck, Burt! Time to eat!" And Burt, winking and blinking his eyelids, comes stumbling down the stairs to breakfast so as not to keep Leela waiting.

Burt Dow has a giggling gull for a pet. Every morning she roosts on the roof of the shed where Burt keeps his fishing gear.

The gull giggles, "Tee-he-he-hee!" until Burt comes out and tosses her a pancake or a popover, or sometimes a piece of cinnamon toast.

When Burt Dow puts out to sea in the *Tidely-Idley*, everybody in town knows it. They hear him pump out all the water that has leaked in overnight, slish-cashlosh, slish-cashlosh! Then there is a pause while Burt checks the tenderest spot—between the pink plank (the color of Ginny Poor's pantry) and the green plank (the color of the floor and doors in Doc Walton's waiting-room).

Then they hear him start the make-and-break engine, clackety *bang!* clackety *bang!* And they see him, firm hand on the tiller, giggling gull flying along behind, heading out of the cove and going clackety-bangety down the bay.

One morning the cock crowed, "Cockety-doodly," and Leela rattled her stove lids klinkety-klink, shouting, "Hit the deck, Burt, time to eat!" And Burt came downstairs winking and blinking his sleepy eyelids and ate his breakfast.

He tossed the giggling gull a popover—"Tee-he-he-hee!"—and went down to the cove to pump out the *Tidely-Idley*, slish-cashlosh, slish-cashlosh.

He gently felt the tender spot between the pink plank (the color of Ginny Poor's pantry) and the green plank (the color of the floor and doors in Doc Walton's waiting-room).

"Giggling gull," he said sadly, "'twon't be long before the *Tidely-Idley* gets planted with geraniums and Indian peas."

Then he started the make-and-break, clackety-BANG! clackety-BANG! And, firm hand on the tiller, giggling gull flying along behind, he headed out of the cove, going clackety-bangety down the bay to fish for cod.

Burt kept studying the color of the sky, the color of the water, and the direction of the wind.

"An old deep-water man like me always keeps a weather eye out," says Burt, "but he keeps *two* weather eyes out when he puts out to sea in a vessel as old and leaky as the *Tidely-Idley!*"

It looked like a good day, so Burt took the *Tidely-Idley* way, way out to the end of the bay and into the open sea. He shut off the make-and-break engine and let the boat drift on the gentle swell. Then he baited up his hook with clams and lowered it over the side to fish for cod.

Burt didn't get any bites, not even a teeny-weeny nibble, so he cranked up the make-and-break and moved the *Tidely-Idley* to another spot.

But there were no fish there either. He didn't even pull up a pollock or a sculpin.

"There must be something down there frightening those fish!" Burt confided to the giggling gull.

"Tee-he-he-hee!" the giggling gull agreed.

Then Burt felt a substantial sort of tug on his line that almost, but not quite, pulled him over the side.

Then Burt pulled . . . and then Burt tugged . . . he heaved and he tugged, he grunted and groaned until the *Tidely-Idley* practically stood on end.

But he couldn't haul in even a single stitch of line.

"Must be caught on the bottom," said Burt.

"Tee-he-he-hee!" The giggling gull was much amused and she teetered on the tip of the tiller to see what would happen next.

Well, Burt, so it seemed, finally got his line uncaught from the bottom and was hauling it in, in a moderate sort of way, not paying much attention, to see if he needed more bait.

The giggling gull was teetering to and fro on the tip of the tiller and tittering "Tee-he-he-hee!" now and then, in a nervous sort of way.

She might have noticed something or other that for that particular moment hadn't come to Burt's attention.

But the *very* next moment it came to Burt's attention that he'd pulled up a

WHALE OF A TAIL!…

Or 'twas t'other-way-around—the tail of a whale had pulled up *Burt!*

Burt grabbed the pump handle and hung on while he swung around, this-a-way, that-a-way. The giggling gull teetered on the tip of the tiller and laughed fit to split.

Burt finally slacked up on the line, or 'twas t'other-way-round—finally the *tail* slacked up on the line. But then the tail began to thrash about, this-a-way, that-a-way, in such a manner as to call Burt's attention to the fact that there was a *whale* on the other end of it.

"Ahoy there, whale!" bellowed Burt. "Hold your horses! Keep your shirt on! Head into the wind and slack off the main sheet!"

The whale couldn't hear because his hearing gear was so far upwind from his steering gear that had come afoul of Burt's cod hook.

"Ahoy there, you giggling gull!" shouted Burt. "Fly away down there and tell this whale that this vessel has a couple of tender places in her planking. He's about to stave us in and send the *Tidely-Idley* and all hands straight to Davy Jones's locker!"

The barb of Burt's cod hook was barely caught in the blubber of the tail, and since it didn't hurt, the whale quieted down and allowed Burt to haul in his cod line cautiously, so he could remove the hook.

When the tail came within reach, Burt had his pliers ready. Working ever so carefully so as not to tickle, he snipped off the barb and eased out the hook.

"There, now!" said Burt. "Only a little bit of a hole, and I've got just the thing for that."

He reached down in the bottom of his tool kit and brought out a box of band-aids Doc Walton had given him (just in case a lobster ever took a nip out of a finger). They were decorated with peppermint stripes, and fortunately they were the kind that stick to *anything*, even *whale tails!*

"There, now, Cap'n Whale!" said Burt proudly. "I'll wager your rudder won't leak out any blubber or take aboard any water and get waterlogged now."

But just then—CA-SMACK! A whopping big wave caught the *Tidely-Idley* in a very embarrassing position and jolted her to the bottom of her keel, all the way from prow to propeller!

Burt had forgotten to keep his weather eyes out, what with getting this poor whale out of all the trouble he was in, and hadn't noticed that it was beginning to blow. ("Tip of his tail snagged on a cod hook—all his blubber 'bout to dribble through the hole! . . .")

Burt started the make-and-break engine and managed to head the *Tidely-Idley* into the wind, but he knew he'd never make it home. However, he did make it to the leeward side of the whale and, with a firm hand on the tiller, giggling gull flying along behind, headed chuggety-bangety up to the bow of the whale to have a face-to-face talk.

"It's blowin' a gale of wind, whale!" bellowed Burt, coming right to the point. "And one good turn deserves another.

"The *Tidely-Idley*'s taking aboard water between those two tender planks. I'm a-pumping just as fast as I can pump, but the water's above the floor boards and 'bout to stall the make-and-break. I'm afeared this vessel and all hands aboard are headed for Davy Jones's locker!

"No doubt the *Tidely-Idley*'d taste terrible," Burt went on, still coming right to the point, "and her barnacled bottom would smart your tongue, whale. The make-and-break would taste bitter as bile, and me, an old deep-water man in oilskins and boots, 'long with this giggling gull, would make gosh-awful trimmings for any meal—*but,*" pleaded Burt, "couldn't you just sort of *swallow* us—temporary, of course—while this gale of wind blows itself out?"

The whale gave a little snort and didn't say anything. Apparently this was a whale of few words. He just opened his mouth wide and said, "AH-H-H!"—in the classic tradition.

Burt set the throttle of the make-and-break at wide open and, chuggeta-bang! chuggeta-bang! firm hand on the tiller, giggling gull flying along behind, guided the *Tidely-Idley* into the whale's mouth and navigated the length of the gullet and into the whale's tummy, without so much as touching a tonsil on the way down!

"Well!" said Burt. "I naturally expected it to be dark inside a whale's tummy, but I didn't expect it to be as dark as this. A few portholes for light and ventilation would improve the design of this animal."

This idea struck the giggling gull as funny, and she started giggling again. Burt was bending over and bumbling about in the dark, trying to find his lantern. He bumped his head on the make-and-break and yelled, "Out of my way, you chuggety, bangafied batch of old iron!"

"Tee-he-he-hee!" This made the giggling gull laugh fit to split.

"Gull," Burt said testily, "some day I'll *gaggle* you! I never realized until now how limited your vocabulary is. You'd be a poor companion to be shipwrecked on a sunny desert island with, and you're even worse in dry dock, down in this dark, damp tummy of a whale. If I had my choice, I'd take a dictionary every time."

Burt had found the lantern and was feeling around, trying to find a dry spot on which to strike a match, when he had a very disquieting thought.

"Supposing this whale didn't hear every word I said out there in that gale of wind?" he asked. "What if he doesn't understand the English language red-letter perfect? Or maybe that he's absent-minded? He might not know, or remember, that we're supposed to be *temporary* guests, so to speak.

"Yup, giggling gull," Burt continued, "we'll have to make sure we get ourselves *unswallowed!*"

He finally struck a match (used the seat of his pants).

"Well!" he said as the light flared up. "I naturally expected *pink* would be the color of this whale's tummy, but I wasn't prepared for pink *identical* with the pink in Ginny Poor's pantry! Yup! Like a big pink cave, that's what it is."

Burt checked over his boat and found that the spot where the wave had slapped the *Tidely-Idley* on her tender bottom would need considerable caulking, patching, and painting. In fact, the water that only moments before had leaked from the ocean *into* the *Tidely-Idley* was now leaking t'other-way-round, out of the *Tidely-Idley* and on to the pink deck of the whale's tummy.

After Burt finished his caulking, patching, and painting, he said, "'Tain't perfect, but she'll hold until we get home, I *hope!*

"Giggling gull, we have to get busy! Leela's back home, rattling her stove lids and getting impatient over our not being home in time to eat!"

First of all, Burt tugged and shoved until he got the *Tidely-Idley* turned about so that her bow pointed in the right direction. *Then* he systematically set about trying to give the whale an upset tummy.

"Whales has got strong stomachs," Burt explained to the giggling gull, "and it takes more than a mixture of catsup and ice cream, pickles and peppermint, mince pie and mustard, to call their attention to the fact that their tummy's upset."

He began by pumping out the *Tidely-Idley* to the very bottom of the bilge. In an old boat, that always produces a lot of interesting things, such as old crab claws, clams, bait, rusty fishhooks, a can opener, corroded pieces of brass, all mixed in with a nice big helping of *sediment*. Burt started scooping up the sediment on the end of a piece of shingle and began flipping a-little-gob-here, a-little-gob-there, making big splatter spots on the lining of the tummy. The tummy began to quiver like a horse's flanks flicking off flies!

Then Burt opened a left-over gallon of yellow deck paint and started sloshing it around, dribbling a-little-bit-here, a-little-bit-there. He was beginning to enjoy himself—probably because it was the first time he'd ever had a chance really to express his personality in paint.

Next he took a can of cup grease and, with the shingle, started spattering a few accents here and there.

By now the whale's tummy was *all* a-quiver! It disturbed Burt's aim a bit, and he misplaced a few blobs of cup grease. Well! The tummy began to make rumbling noises and flip-a-lot this-a-way, flip-a-lot that-a-way, and Burt knew right off that it would take only the littlest touch to make the tummy break loose from its moorings and get upset.

He, quick as he could, jumped into the *Tidely-Idley* and started the make-and-break, chuggety-*bang!* chuggety-*bang!*

"Giggling gull!" he shouted. "Wiggle your wings and fly away up into the for'ard hatchway and tickle this whale's throat with a feather!"

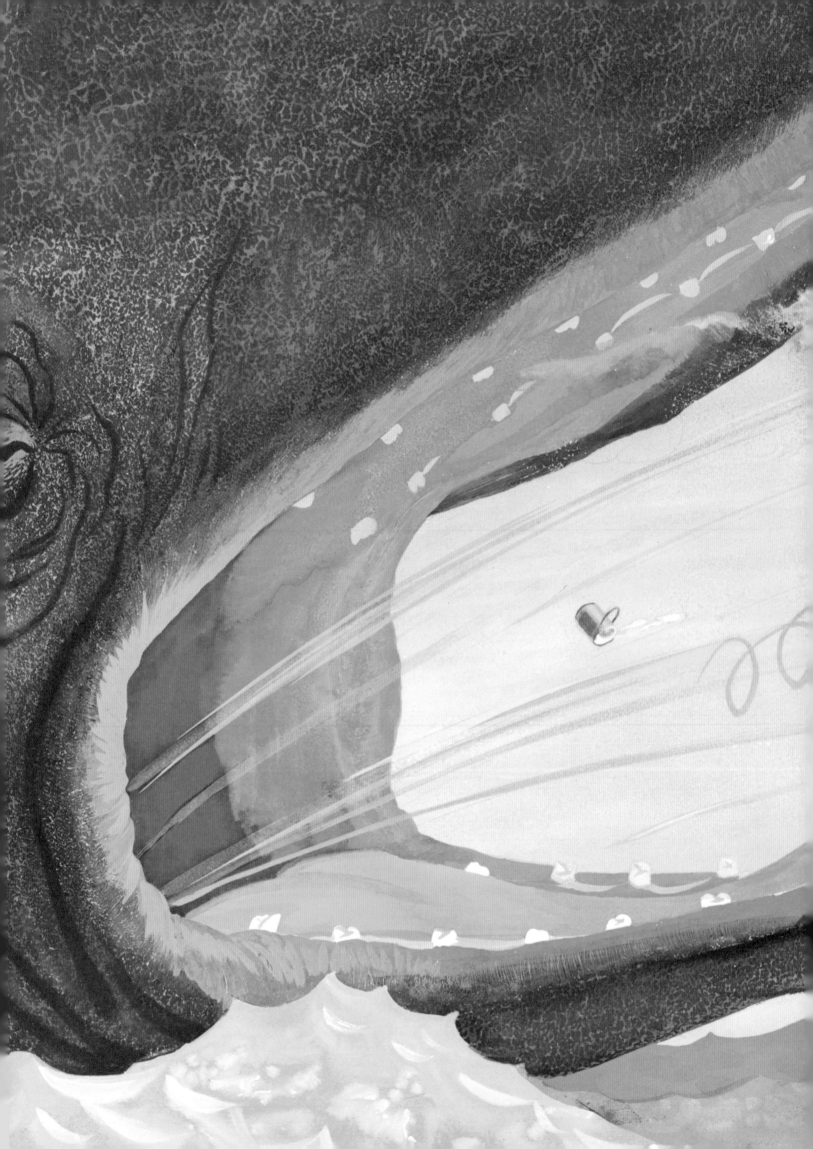

Of course the exhaust and jiggling of the
make-and-break helped, but 'twas the tickle that
turned the trick! With the dark dampest rumble
ever heard, the big tummy flipped this-a-way,
that-a-way, and then with a whale of a "BURP!"
boat and Burt, firm hand on the tiller, giggling
gull flying along behind, make-and-break going
wide open, came clackety-bangety out of the wide
open mouth of the whale, going so fast that they
barely touched the tops of the first two waves and
landed right dab

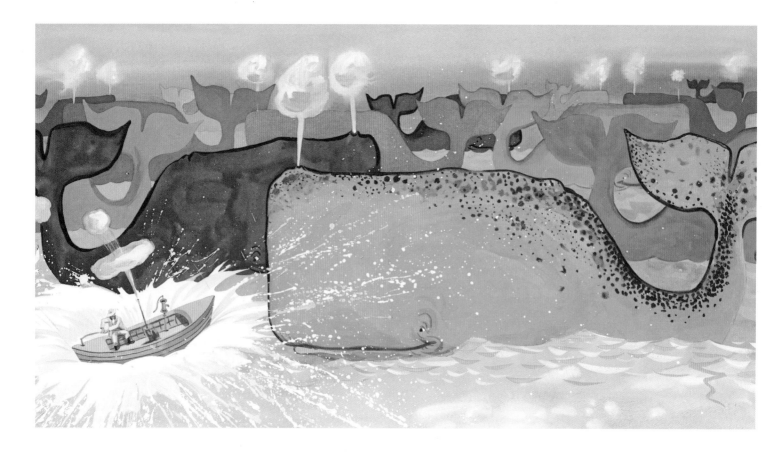

SMACK! in the middle of a whole school of whales! Burt eased up on the throttle of the make-and-break and tried to steer a snug course between the two whale-tails, one the color of Ginny Poor's pantry, t'other the color of the floors and doors in Doc Walton's waiting-room, but the way was blocked by a whale-tail the color of the porch and trim on Cap'n Haskell's house. Every time Burt shifted course, there seemed to be more whale-tails in the way. Finally Burt stopped the make-and-break and let the *Tidely-Idley* drift among the whale-tails while he decided what to do next.

He bobbed around in his boat, studying the situation. Then he took out his glass and studied some more. Then he finally said, "Well!!! That's a whale of a lot of whale-tails"—making what amounted to a classic understatement. "You can hardly see the forest for the trees," Burt complained, "or the whales for the tails!"

There must be some reason, thought Burt, why all this school of whales are waving their tails toward the *Tidely-Idley*.

"All except one," he added, peeping through his glass at a pale whale that looked exactly as though it had an upset tummy from a bit of bilge-water, cup grease, deck paint, and having its throat tickled by a feather. "Yup! That whale looks a bit under the weather, but it also looks *contented*."

But meanwhile the rest of the school of whales seemed to be getting impatient. They twitched the tips of their tails and *whacked* them down on the water.

"Careful!" bellowed Burt. "The *Tidely-Idley*'s got a tender spot, and you're apt to spring a seam—if first you don't swat us like a fly, which is no fit way for an old deep-water man and his vessel to go to Davy Jones."

What with the *Tidely-Idley*'s regular leaks, and all the water being splashed aboard by impatient whale-tails, Burt had to keep pumping, slish-cashlosh, slish-cashlosh, and he didn't have much time to wonder what made one whale contented and what made all the

rest of the school so slap-happy with their tails. Stronger and younger men might have given up, but not our deep-water man, Burt Dow! He kept right on pumping with one hand, slish-cashlosh, slish-cashlosh, while he poked around in his tool box with the other. Still pumping, slish-cashlosh, slish-cashlosh, he pulled out a band-aid, unfurled it from its wrappings between his teeth, and slapped it onto the tip of the nearest whale-tail.

Burt knew right off that his troubles were over.

"The whales were only impatient at my taking so long to understand 'em," Burt explained to the giggling gull. "Whales is really very patient about standing or swimming in line to have the tips of their tails decked out with a band-aid."

After all the whale-tails had been decorated, each with a peppermint-striped band-aid, the entire school swam, tails held high, in a tremendous circle around the *Tidely-Idley*.

An old deep-water man like Burt couldn't resist shouting, "Thar she blows!" in the best classic tradition.

Then all together, *one, two, three,* the school of whales blew three big blows for Burt Dow and swam off over the horizon.

"I never did see," said Burt, "so many tons of contentment come from out of such a little old band-aid box!"

He still had one band-aid left, and he knew he'd never need it himself—never was a lobster hatched or catched as could ever clamp a claw on Burt Dow—so just for a joke he said, "Giggling gull, let's take this last band-aid home to Leela!"

"Tee-he-he-hee!" giggled the gull, because she always was one who enjoyed Burt's little jokes.

"And we'd better take it right now," said Burt, "so's not to keep her waiting."

But then he noticed that the water was up over the floor boards. So he started pumping again, slish-cashlosh, slish-cashlosh! Then he cranked the make-and-break, clackety-BANG! clackety-BANG! and with a firm hand on the tiller, giggling gull flying along behind, he headed the *Tidely-Idley* back up the bay.

They made it home just as the cock began to crow.

LENTIL

1940

In the town of Alto, Ohio, there lived a boy named Lentil.

Lentil had a happy life except for one thing—he wanted to sing, but he couldn't!

It was most embarrassing, because when he opened his mouth to try, only strange sounds came out. . . .

And he couldn't even whistle because he couldn't pucker his lips.

But he did want to make music, so he saved up enough pennies to buy a harmonica.

Lentil was proud of his new harmonica and he decided to become an expert. So he played a lot, whenever and wherever he could.

His favorite place to practice was in the bathtub, because there the tone was improved one hundred per cent.

He used to play almost all the way to school. Down Vine Street to the corner of Main, past the finest house in Alto, which belonged to the great Colonel Carter. Then . . .

past the drug store, the barber shop, and the Alto Library, which was a gift of the great Colonel Carter,

by the Methodist Church, through the Carter Memorial Park, and around the Soldiers and Sailors Monument that the Colonel had built there.

Then Lentil would
stuff his harmonica into his
pocket and take a short cut up
the alley behind the hardware store
so he would not be late for school.

People would smile and wave hello to Lentil as he walked down the street, because everyone in Alto liked Lentil's music; that is, everybody but Old Sneep. Old Sneep didn't like much of anything or anybody. He just sat on a park bench and whittled and grumbled.

One day the news got around that the great Colonel Carter, who had been away for two years, was coming home. People began to plan a grand welcome, but when Old Sneep heard the news he said: "Humph! We wuz boys together. He ain't a mite better'n you or me and he needs takin' down a peg or two." Sneep just kept right on whittling, but everybody else kept right on planning. Colonel Carter was the town's most important citizen, so . . .

the people hung out flags and decorated the streets. The mayor prepared a speech, the Alto Brass Band put on their new uniforms, and the printer, the grocer, the plumber, the minister, the barber, the druggist, the ice man, the school teachers, the housewives and their husbands and their children—yes,

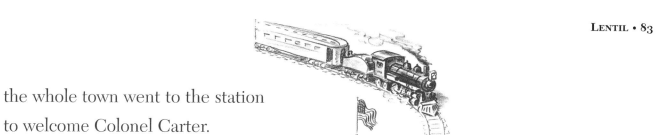

the whole town went to the station
to welcome Colonel Carter.

The train pulled in. The musicians in the band were waiting for the leader to
signal them to play, the leader was waiting for the mayor to nod to him to start
the band, and the mayor was waiting for Colonel Carter
to step from his private car. All the people held their
breath and waited.

Then there was a wet sound from above.

There sat Old Sneep, sucking on a lemon.

Old Sneep knew that when the musicians looked at him their mouths would pucker up so they could not play their horns. The whole band looked up at Old Sneep. The mayor gave the signal to play, but the cornetist couldn't play his cornet, the piccolo player couldn't play his piccolo, the trombone player couldn't play his trombone, and the tuba player couldn't play his tuba, because their lips were all puckered up.

They couldn't play a single note! The musicians just stood there holding their instruments and looking up at Sneep sucking on the lemon. The leader looked helpless, the people were too surprised to move or say a thing, and the mayor wrung his hands and wore a look that said: "Can't somebody do something, please!"

As Colonel Carter stepped from his car, the only sound was the noise of Sneep's lemon.

Clouds began to gather on the colonel's brow and he said: "Hmph" in an indignant sort of way.

Of course Lentil's lips were not puckered and he knew that something had to be done. So he took out his harmonica and started to play "Comin' 'round the Mountain When She Comes."

When Lentil began to play the second chorus, Colonel Carter smiled.

Then he let out a loud chuckle and began to sing "Driving Six White Horses When She Comes."

Then everybody sang and they all marched down Main Street behind the colonel's car.

Lentil rode with the colonel, who took a turn at the harmonica when Lentil's wind began to give out. (He said that he hadn't played one since he was a boy, but he did very well considering.)

They marched to the colonel's house and paraded through the gate and onto the front lawn. The mayor's committee served ice cream cones to all the citizens and Colonel Carter made a speech saying how happy he was about such a fine welcome and how happy he was to be home again. When he said that he was going to build a new hospital for the town of Alto, everybody was happy—even Old Sneep!

So you never can tell what will happen when you learn to play the harmonica.

Ever So Much More So

from

CENTERBURG TALES

1951

The early afternoon spring sunshine came peeping into the lunchroom and reflected off the stainless steel trim of Uncle Ulysses' unpredictable automatic doughnut machine.

The sun reflected off the shiny metal and right into the eyes of Uncle Ulysses, who was settled comfortably at the counter, having an after-lunch chat with the sheriff and the judge.

Uncle Ulysses blinked his eyes and thought, "I'll have to get up and go all the way outside to wind that awning down. Ought to put a motor on it," he thought, "with a button under the counter, to save all those steps and all the winding." Then he yawned out loud and shifted his position just enough to allow the reflection to go over his shoulder.

"Put a button on it," he said, thinking out loud, much to the confusion of the judge and the sheriff.

"Put what?" asked Homer, who was wiping crumbs off the counter.

"Oh, yes, Homer," said Uncle Ulysses with a start. "Put the awning down, like a good fellow, would you please?"

"Okay, Uncle Ulysses," said Homer and, after wiping a pile of crumbs off the counter into his apron, he hustled outside and shook them onto the curb. He watched while the Centerburg town-hall pigeons started arriving to eat crumbs, then hustled back across the walk and wound down the awning.

"Thank you, Homer," said Uncle Ulysses as Homer came back into the lunchroom.

"Everything look feacepul—I mean peaceful—and law abidin' out on the square?" the sheriff demanded of Homer.

"Dulcy Dooner is headed in this direction," Homer said.

"Ah-h!" said the judge. "*That* exceedingly uncooperative citizen of our community!"

They all turned and watched through the window of the lunchroom while Dulcy paused next to the monument. The sheriff bristled when Dulcy struck a match on the bronze tablet, casually lit his pipe, and flipped the burned match in the general direction of the statue of "Peace." Then he came on toward the lunchroom, detouring slightly in order to scuffle through the crumbs and frighten a few pigeons.

Slam! went the door of the lunchroom as Dulcy came in. But the sheriff, the judge, Uncle Ulysses, and Homer hardly jumped. They all knew how Dulcy closed doors.

"What are you up to these days, Dulcy?" asked the sheriff, eying Dulcy carefully as though expecting to find something like packages of strange seeds or bottles of elixir sticking out of his pockets.

"Always suspectin' me!" complained Dulcy. "Sheriff, you're the most suspicious guy in the state of Ohio!"

"In view of several unfortunate occurrences attributable directly to certain actions of one Dulcy Dooner, I am of the opinion," the judge proclaimed in his usual pompous way, "that the suspicions of our sheriff are entirely justified."

"Good afternoon, my friends!" said a strange voice, and the judge, the sheriff, Uncle Ulysses, Dulcy Dooner, and Homer turned to see a stranger walk in the door. He had a case under one arm and a folding stand under the other.

"Good afternoon, my friends," he repeated. "You are without doubt the most fortunate people in the world—and in just one minute, yes, one short sixty seconds of your valuable time, I am going to make you even more fortunate . . . thankful that I have come to you with this sensational introductory offer!"

The stranger, after introducing himself as Professor Ear, "Professor Atmos *P. H.* Ear," talked on and on, scarcely stopping to take a breath, and at the same time managed to shut the door, tip his hat, unfold his stand, set up his case carefully, and take off his gloves, smiling sweetly all the while.

"I have in here," he continued, tapping the lid of his case, "one of the wonders of the world! Yes, my friends, and you *are* my very good friends, in just one minute I am going to reveal to you a product and make you an offer that will change your life, *if* you are the kind of people that get a *bang* out of life," he exclaimed, emphasizing the *bang* with a flourish and swat of his gloves on top of his case. "You are the ones, yes, the very people, that will have the good sense, the intelligence, imagination, ability, good judgment, and love of the finer things in life to apply this amazing product to obtain the beneficial blessings, the sense of well being, and complete, yes, complete, satisfaction that this remarkable product has the ability to impart to each and every one."

"We don't want any o'—" Dulcy started to interrupt.

"*It is my honor,*" continued the professor, loud enough to be heard above Dulcy's interruption, "to bring to you this fabulously amazing and most phenomenal product, and its name is"—he paused dramatically, snapping free the fastenings of the case and throwing up the cover—"its name is Eversomuch More-so!"

The judge, the sheriff, Uncle Ulysses, Dulcy, and Homer all stared at the cans displayed so suddenly before their eyes.

"What—?" Uncle Ulysses started to ask.

"Ah-h, *what?*" echoed the stranger. "Ah-h, yes, my good friends, I can see the question in your friendly faces. *What* is this remarkable Eversomuch More-so, and *what* can this phenomenal Eversomuch More-so do for *me?* In just one minute, just thirty short seconds, I am going to demonstrate to you and to prove to you without the shadow of a doubt that this product can accomplish wondrous things.

"Each and every can," said the professor, picking up a can and continuing without a pause, "yes, *each* and *every* can comes complete with a handy adjustable top. A slight twist to either left or right opens the tiny holes in the cap, making EVERSOMUCH MORE-SO readily accessible for instantaneous application.

"Now for the purposes of our demonstration," the professor continued quickly, "we shall use these delicious-looking doughnuts. Young man," he said to Homer, "if you will be so kind as to pass the tray, and if you gentlemen," he requested, bowing low, "would be so kind as to take two doughnuts . . ."

While Homer passed the tray and everyone took two doughnuts, one in each hand, the professor said, "Now, my friends, we are ready to—uht, uht, sonny, don't forget me!" And before Homer could pass the tray the professor speared two dough-nuts on the end of his cane.

The judge and Uncle Ulysses exchanged looks, and the sheriff was about to ask, "When—?"

"*Now*," said the professor loudly, banging on his case for undivided attention, "now we are ready to proceed with our demonstration. Yes, in just one minute, only sixty seconds—but first," said the professor, picking up a can of EVERSOMUCH MORE-SO, "I shall acquaint you with this wondrous product."

The judge, the sheriff, Uncle Ulysses, Homer, and Dulcy all leaned closer, each with both eyes watching the professor twist the adjustable can top, and each with doughnuts in both hands.

"As I proceed, young man," the professor said to Homer, "please pour cups of your delicious coffee for everyone here."

"Ahuumph!" the judge cleared his throat restlessly.

"A cup of coffee costs—" Uncle Ulysses began.

"Everybody eat the doughnut in his right hand!" the professor commanded loudly. "Delicious—uhm-m? Simply delicious," he declared, taking a dainty bite from the one on the tip of his cane. Having safely stopped all interruptions with large bites of doughnut, the professor continued in a low, confiding voice, "EVERSOMUCH MORE-SO is a truly remarkable product."

He shook some on his doughnut and swung it in front of the noses of his audience, on the tip of his cane, for all to see. "Remarkable, you say!" interpreted the professor, loudly enough to be heard over sounds coming from behind mouthfuls of doughnut. "Yes, my friends, EVERSOMUCH MORE-SO is *invisible!* And what's more, EVERSOMUCH MORE-SO cannot be smelled," he said, passing the can quickly beneath every nose. "You cannot feel it, and you cannot see it," he added, rubbing his fingertips and then wiggling the can close to his ear.

"Pass the coffee, young man!" he commanded Homer and quickly continued his speech. "EVERSOMUCH MORE-SO is *absolutely invisible* to the naked eye, odorless to the human nose, soundless to the—young man, don't forget the cream and sugar—as I was saying, soundless to the unassisted perceptibilities of the human ear, undetected, by itself, by the sensitive human nerves of touch, and what is more, EVERSOMUCH MORE-SO, taken from the can in its natural unadulterated state, is completely tasteless to the sensitive taste buds of the human tongue.

"Now you are about to ask," the professor said, "why should we be interested in this product we cannot see, smell, taste, hear, or feel? But *watch closely!* Sprinkle a small amount of EVERSOMUCH MORE-SO in your good aromatic cup of coffee—so! *Immediately*, yes, my friends, *im-me-e-ediately*, that good aromatic cup of coffee becomes *ever so much more so!* Yes, indeed, and after sprinkling a few drops of this remarkable, invisible, tasteless, odorless, textureless, absolutely soundless product on the delicious doughnut you hold in your hand, that delicious doughnut becomes immediately *ever so much more so* delicious!"

The can was passed to Dulcy and on to the judge, from the judge to the sheriff, on to Uncle Ulysses, and last of all to Homer. Everyone shook out a small amount of EVERSOMUCH MORE-SO into his cup of coffee and onto his second doughnut.

Everybody began tasting carefully, exchanging glances, tasting once more, and nodding solemnly, while the professor talked on and on.

"Yes, my friends, that is indeed the most *ever so much more so* delicious doughnut and the best, yes, without doubt, the most *ever so much more so* aromatic cup of coffee you have ever tasted."

Everyone was nodding in agreement and enjoying his doughnut and coffee—everybody but Homer, who was tasting his coffee and making miserable faces. Finally he asked, "What if you don't like coffee? Does—?"

"Does EVERSOMUCH MORE-SO work on *everything*, this young man wants to know?" the professor said quickly. "Ah, but yes!" he shouted. "*Everything*. It will make a rose smell ever so much more lovely, curly hair ever so much more curly, beautiful music ever so much more beautiful. Yes, my friends, surely you are all intelligent enough to realize the far-reaching possibilities of EVERSOMUCH MORE-SO! It comes to you in this convenient can, put up under the most sanitary conditions by the famous Doctor Forscyth Eversomuch in his great open-air laboratory. One can, yes, one single can, lasts a lifetime. After purchasing one can of EVERSOMUCH MORE-SO, a man can rest assured that he will never again want for another can of EVERSOMUCH MORE-SO. It will keep just as fresh, just as free from impurities, just as potent inside the can as the day it was packed. And now for the amazing price of fifty cents, only four bits, one-half of one dollar, a lifetime can of EVERSOMUCH MORE-SO is yours. This is one of the good things of the earth, men. Now don't miss this golden opportunity to own a convenient can of it for this amazing price of fifty cents."

The sheriff counted out fifty cents, the judge bought a can, so did Uncle Ulysses. Even Dulcy borrowed half a dollar from the judge and bought a can.

As the professor prepared to snap shut his case Homer asked, "If you don't like coffee and you put EVERSOMUCH MORE-SO in it, then will you not like coffee *ever so much more so*?"

"How would you like," the professor asked, "a nice fast kick—eherump—would you like a nice free can of EVERSOMUCH MORE-SO?" And he quickly tossed a can to Homer, snapped up his case, hooked his cane over his arm, pulled on his gloves, tipped his hat, and was out of the door and away in an instant.

"G'by," said Dulcy abruptly. "I'm gonna try this stuff on something."

"Me too," said the sheriff.

"Good day, Ulysses," said the judge, remembering to be polite.

"Um-m," answered Uncle Ulysses absent-mindedly, for he was carefully selecting two doughnuts.

When he and Homer were alone Uncle Ulysses put the two doughnuts on two plates.

One he left plain and the other he sprinkled liberally with EVERSOMUCH MORE-SO. Then he tasted, first one, then the other, the one with, the other without. He stroked his chin, then called Homer, and they both tasted.

"I'll be durned," said Uncle Ulysses finally.

"You know, Uncle Ulysses," Homer said, "nobody paid for coffee and doughnuts this afternoon."

"I'll be durned," Uncle Ulysses repeated. *"Ever so much more so!"*

The following Thursday Uncle Ulysses sat slumped on his stool behind the counter when the judge walked in.

"Judge," Uncle Ulysses asked sleepily, "do you notice anything different about me?"

The judge looked Uncle Ulysses over carefully and said, "I notice a marked tendency toward sleepiness."

"Uh-uh-uh," nodded Uncle Ulysses with a yawn, "that's what Aggie says. Says I'm lazier than ever—*ever so much more so*, she says. That's not so, Judge. But I just can't seem to sleep at night any more. I put some EVERSOMUCH MORE-SO on my inner-spring mattress to make it softer."

"And did it?" asked the judge.

"Yes," nodded Uncle Ulysses, "but I spilled some of the stuff on one of the springs that had a slight squeak and it seemed to start squeaking *ever so much more so*. Can't sleep a wink in that bed. Hello, Sheriff," he added as the sheriff came in, looking flustered and red in the face.

"Gentlemen," the judge said solemnly, "I fear that some grave metamorphosis of cerebral or of physical characteristics has erupted within my innermost self. In fact," he said pompously, "I am just exactly like myself, only *ever so much more so*."

"Tomesimes," said the sheriff sadly, "I wix my mords all up, but sis thuff ixxes 'em mup so I don't even snow what I'm krying to snay!"

"I think," said Uncle Ulysses gravely, "that we are imaginin' the whole thing. A man just *can't* be more like himself than he is already. Let's ask Dulcy," suggested Uncle Ulysses.

And indeed there was Dulcy, stamping across the grass in the square. He stumbled over a "Keep Off the Grass" sign, let out a loud bellow, picked up the sign and threw it in the general direction of "Peace." "Peace" went kabonk! as the sign smacked into her. After knocking over a trash can, Dulcy came on toward the lunchroom.

"He's *ever so much more so*, all right. Been eatin' it every day, I bet," said Uncle Ulysses while the sheriff and judge nodded.

Slam! went the door as Dulcy came in. Homer and Freddy came in soon after and looked concernedly at ever so drowsy Uncle Ulysses, at the ever so pompous judge, the ever so flustered and suspicious sheriff, and the *ever so much more so* uncooperative citizen named Dulcy Dooner.

"How *you* feelin', Homer?" Uncle Ulysses asked.

"Just fine, Uncle Ulysses," Homer answered. "You look sleepy, Uncle Ulysses. Got spring fever?"

"What did you do with your can of EVERSOMUCH MORE-SO, Homer?" asked Uncle Ulysses, trying to keep awake and unconcerned.

"Oh, *that* stuff," said Homer. "Freddy and I put a lot of it on my radio to improve the reception. It seemed a little better but it seemed to make ever so much more static and interference too. So we took a screw driver and pried the top off the EVERSOMUCH MORE-SO can, just to see what was inside."

"Yes?" everybody asked.

"Yes," said Homer.

"It was empty," Freddy said with a shrug.

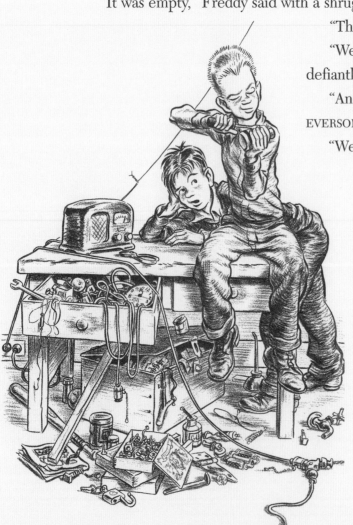

"That stuff is invisible," Dulcy reminded.

"Well, it was an empty can!" said Freddy defiantly.

"And what could be more empty than an EVERSOMUCH MORE-SO empty can?" asked Homer.

"We've been dindled, doggonit—I mean swindled," howled the sheriff.

"Our fertile imaginations have led us astray," pronounced the judge.

"The professor took us, all right," chuckled Uncle Ulysses, seeming to come more awake of a sudden.

"Here, Judge," said Dulcy, handing over his can of EVERSOMUCH MORE-SO. "Now we're even and I don't owe you fifty cents."

"Help yourselves to doughnuts, boys," Uncle Ulysses said solicitously, the way he always did before asking a favor.

"Boys," he said, "we can't let this affair come to the attention of Grampa Hercules or we'll never hear the end of it."

Homer hesitated until both he and Freddy had helped themselves to doughnuts and then said, "He already knows."

"What?" cried the sheriff and Uncle Ulysses.

"Yep. I put the top back on the can and decided to give it to Grampa Herc. It's the sort of thing he would appreciate ever so much, you know," Homer said.

"And what did the gold oat—I mean, what did the *old goat* say?" demanded the sheriff, clearly expecting the worst.

"He said it beat all what the world was coming to, didn't he, Freddy? And he said," Homer continued, "that it used to come in bulk when he was young, and lots cheaper too. Nobody bothered to give it a fancy name or put it in a package with an adjustable top."

"Continue, young man," the judge suggested.

"Well," Homer said, "he allowed as how he'd never tried this *packaged* kind of EVERSOMUCH MORE-SO and he had a feeling he'd like to see if it was just as strong as the old-fashioned kind. So I sold him *my* can for a dollar."

"That's my nephew, and more so," said Uncle Ulysses.

"We been swindled!" repeated the sheriff. "I shoulda locked that fella up!"

"*Entirely* outside the law!" the judge proclaimed.

"Helloooo, everybody!" said Grampa Hercules, letting himself in the door.

Uncle Ulysses sighed and wondered to himself how more so Grampa Herc could possibly get.

"How do you feel, Hercules?" the judge inquired.

"Never felt so good in my whole life!" answered Grampa Herc.

"Okay, what did you do with it?" demanded Dulcy.

Grampa Herc looked puzzled; then he said, "Oh, you mean the stuff in the can, the EVERSOMUCH MORE-SO. Wu-a-ll, you know, I got to

thinkin'. An old fella like me ain't got long to spend in these parts. I can use up a lot o' time sprinklin' a bit on this and that, here and there. I thought to myself, what's one big, all-fired-honest-to-crawfish, powerful, important way to use up a lifetime supply of EVERSOMUCH MORE-SO? I thought and I thought, and finally it come to me. I went out in my backyard and hunted up a nice soft spot of black earth. Then I started to shake that stuff on that wonderful earth as hard as my arm could shake. I shook until my arm got tired, and I reckon the can was just about empty. Then I took a screw driver and pried off the lid and poured the EVERSOMUCH MORE-SO can full of water, and *do you know*, that was the *dampest*, the *soakenest*, wringin' wettest sloppin'-to-goodness can of water I ever laid eyes on!"

"Yes?" said Uncle Ulysses.

"Yep!" said Grampa Herc. "And then I dumped that EVERSOMUCH MORE-SO soakingest water onto that good old earth and watched it soak in, right down to the core—somewhere halfway between here and China. Then I looked around me and noticed how green the grass looked—trees budding, birds singing, and I felt good all over! See, look out there in the square—just like I'm tellin' you. It's a great old world!" shouted Grampa Herc, leaping up and clicking his heels, "and what's more, it's getting better all the time! So long, everybody!"

Uncle Ulysses, the sheriff, the judge, Dulcy, Homer, and Freddy all walked out into the square in the nice warm spring sunshine.

"Do you think I ought to give this fifty cents back to Grampa Herc?" asked Homer, holding out half a dollar.

"You just loan that to me, Homer," said Dulcy, making a grab, "and I'll buy my can back from the judge. You can owe Grampa Hercules the *other* fifty cents."

"Homer," said Uncle Ulysses, "run back to the lunchroom and bring a screw driver from the tool box. Freddy, you go along and bring a pitcher of water."

Uncle Ulysses was scraping up a nice soft absorbent spot under an old maple right near the statue of "Peace."

"You know," he said, "it's really a waste of time to shake it on. We'll just fill it right up to the top and let it keep a-runnin' over and soakin' in!"

TIME OF
WONDER

1957

Out on the islands that poke their rocky shores above the waters of Penobscot Bay, you can watch the time of the world go by, from minute to minute, hour to hour, from day to day, season to season.

You can watch a cloud peep over the Camden Hills, thirty miles away across the bay—see it slowly grow and grow as it comes nearer and nearer; see it darken the hills with its shadow; and then, see it darken, one after the other, Islesboro, Western Island, Pond Island, Hog Island, Spectacle Island, Two Bush Island—darken all the islands in between, until you, on your island, are standing in the shadow, watching the rain begin to spill down way across the bay.

The rain comes closer and closer. Now you hear a million splashes. Now you even see

the drops on the water . . .
on the age-old rocky point . . .

on the bayberry . . .

on the grass . . .

Now take a breath—

IT'S RAINING ON *YOU!*

At the water's edge on a foggy morning in the early spring you feel as though you were standing alone on the edge of nowhere.

You hear a snorting sound from out of the nowhere and you know that no, you are not alone. A family of porpoises is nearby, rolling over and over, having an acrobatic breakfast of herring under the bay.

Then through the fog you hear Harry Smith over at Blastow's Cove start the engine of his lobster boat and go out to pull his traps.

Suddenly there is a ripple and a splash along the shore that makes you jump! It is the wake from Harry Smith's lobster boat, and you smile because you almost got wet feet that time!

The ripple disappears into the fog, and though you cannot see it you know that it is silently gliding, gliding on its way. Then another distant, unseen splash—and the gulls and cormorants on Two Bush Ledge, with their seabird sense of humor, start giggling and laughing because they too were suddenly surprised by the wake.

Back from the shore the trees look like ghosts. The forest is so quiet that you can hear an insect boring a tunnel deep inside a log. And that other sound—not the beating of your heart, but the one like half a whisper—is the sound of growing ferns, pushing aside dead leaves, unrolling their fiddle-heads, slowly unfurling, slowly stretching.

Now the fog turns yellow. The bees begin to buzz, and a hummingbird hums by. Then all the birds begin to sing, and suddenly the fog has lifted!

And suddenly you find that
you are singing too,

With the blue water sparkling
all around, all around,
With the blue water sparkling
all around!

At the height of the summer
season the bay is spotted with
boats—with racing sailboats,
with cruising schooners, with
busy fishing boats, and with
buzzing outboards.

In the afternoon you sail among the islands, pushed by gentle breezes. You sail
close by Swain's Cove Ledges, where a mother seal is nursing her baby.

And then at sunset, with porpoises puffing and playing around your boat, you
come about and set a course for the island that is home.

The rock on the point of the island is very old. It was fiery hot when the world was new. It was icy cold when a glacier covered it with grinding weight.

This morning the rock is warm in the sun, and loud with happy noise of children who have come to spend the day.

They dive off the rock and swim, then stretch out, dripping, in the sun, making salty young silhouettes on the old scars made by the glacier.

In the afternoon, when the tide is out, they build a castle out of rocks and driftwood below the spot where they had belly-whoppered and dog-paddled during the morning.

In the evening, when the tide is high again, and all your guests have gone, you row around to the point, feeling lonely, until an owl asks a question. A heron croaks an answer.

A seal sniffs softly as he recognizes you, and eider ducks and fishhawks—all are listening, all are watching as you row. By the rock, you shine a light down into the water. There is a crab on the bottom where you were playing this afternoon.

He tiptoes sideways through the castle gate and disappears into its watery keep.

You snap off the light and row toward the dock as the stars are gazing down, their reflections gazing up. In the quiet of the night one hundred pairs of eyes are watching you, while one pair of eyes is watching over all.

As the days grow shorter and shorter there are fewer and fewer boats on the bay, until at last only the fishing boats are left. The wind blows brisk from the northwest, rustling the birch leaves.

The ferns change from green to yellow to brown. The robins are gone from the lawn and the garden. The swallows have flown from their nests in the boathouse.

To take their places, migrating birds from the north stop off to rest on their way south. The crows and the gulls fly over, fussing and feuding. And the hummingbirds visit the petunia patch.

Mr. Billings flies over, looking for schools of herring. When he sees you waving on the beach, he dips the seaplane's wings in greeting.

On some days the wind is so strong that not even the sturdy fishing boats are out on the bay.

Now is the time for being watchful.

And other times there is not a breath of wind to ripple the reflection of an unusual sky.

Now is the time for being prepared.

Over in Blastow's Cove, Harry Smith looks at the sky and says, "We're going to have some weather."

On Eggamoggin Reach, Clyde Snowman listens to the loons and says, "It's a comin'!"

On Cape Rosier, Ferd Clifford listens to the sound of the bell off Spectacle Island and says, "She's gonna blow."

On your island you feel the light crisp feeling go out of the air and a heavy stillness take its place. It's time to make a quick trip to the mainland for food and gasoline.

It's time to get ready.

We're going to have some weather.

It's a-comin'.

She's gonna blow.

In Bucks Harbor are the cruise schooners—the *Alice Wentworth*, the *Stephen Taber*, and the *Victory Chimes*—riding at anchor to spend the winter. Men are busy putting out extra anchors, pulling up skiffs and rowboats, checking moorings, checking chains, checking pennants, getting ready.

Take aboard groceries. Take aboard gasoline. All of the talk is of hundred-pound anchors, two-inch rope, one-inch chain, and will it hold? And the weather . . . and when? Mr. Gray strokes his chin and says, "With the next shift of the tide."

Hurry for home, for there's much to be done before the tide is too low.

The ledges behind Pumpkin Island are covered with gulls, all sitting solemnly faced in the same direction. There is no giggling and cackling as your wake splashes the ledge today. This is no time for seabird sense of humor.

We're going to have some weather.

It's a-comin'.

She's gonna blow.

With the next shift of the tide.

Home on the island, you pull in the sailboat, chain the motorboat fast to its mooring, pull the rowboats high off the beach.

Mr. Smith hurries by with a boatload of lobster traps that he has been taking up.

Over in Swain's Cove, Mr. Billings puts extra lines on the wings of his seaplane.

Fishermen put extra lines on herring boats and scalloping boats.

At Franky Day's boat yard up Benjamin River, and at Hal Vaughn's boat yard up Horseshoe Creek, men are working with the tide pulling up sloops and yawls, ketches and motorboats; shackling chains, tying ropes, making things fast, battening down, getting ready.

Stack the groceries on kitchen shelves. Bring in wood to build a fire. Fill the generator with gas. Then take one last careful look, while the calm sea pauses at dead low water.

A mouse nibbles off one last stalk from the garden and drags it into his mouse hole. A spider scurries across his web and disappears into a knothole. All living things wait, while the first surge of the incoming tide ripples past Eagle Island, ripples past Dirigo, past Pickering, past Two Bush Island. The bell-buoy off Spectacle Island sways slightly with the ripple,

tolling . . .

tolling . . .

tolling the shift of the tide.

Gently at first the wind begins to blow. Gently at first the rain begins to fall.

Suddenly the wind whips the water into sharp, choppy waves. It tears off the sharp tops and slashes them into ribbons of smoky spray. And the rain comes slamming down. The wind comes in stronger and stronger gusts. A branch snaps from a tree.

A gull flies over, flying backward, hoping for a chance to drop into the lee of the island. Out in the channel a tardy fishing boat wallows in the waves, seeking the shelter of Bucks Harbor.

A tree snaps. Above the roar of the hurricane you see and feel but do not hear it fall. A latch gives way. People and papers and parcheesi games are puffed hair-over-eyes across the floor, while Father pushes and strains to close and bolt out the storm.

Mother reads a story, and the words are spoken and lost in the scream of the wind.

You are glad it is a story you have often heard before. Then you all sing together, shouting *"eyes have seen the glory"* just as loud as you can SHOUT. With dish-towels tucked by doorsills just to keep the salt spray out.

The moon comes out, making a rainbow in the salt spray, a promise that the storm will soon be over. Now the wind is lessening, singing loud chords in the treetops. Lessening, it hums as you go up to bed.

And the great swells coming in from the open sea say SH-h-h-h . . . SH-h-h-h . . . SH-h-h-h as they foam over the old rock on the point. Lessening, the wind whispers a lullaby in the spruce branches as you fall asleep in the bright moonlight.

The next morning you awaken to an unaccustomed light made by a frosty coating of salt on all the windows. And out-of-doors in the gentle morning lie reminders of yesterday's hurricane. Fallen and broken trees are everywhere—on the terrace, on the path—blocking your way at every turn. You cannot walk on familiar paths and trails, but you can explore the tops of giant fallen trees, and walk on trunks and limbs where no one ever walked before.

Then, seeking out still more places where no one ever walked before, you explore the jagged holes left by roots of fallen trees. Under an old tree by the house you

discover an Indian shell heap, and, poking in the thousands of snow-white clam shells, so old they crumble at a touch, you realize that you are standing on a place where Indian children stood before the coming of white men.

Now it is time for one last chore of hauling seaweed from the beach to fertilize the garden. Spreading the seaweed with its iodine smell, you are pleased to see that the storm-flattened sunflowers are once more lifting faces to the sun. And here are the hummingbirds, humming a hymn to the morning, making a final round to the last of the petunias. It is time for hummingbirds to leave the island.

It is the end of another summer. It is time for you to leave the island too. Good-by to clams and mussels and barnacles, to crows and swallows, gulls and owls, to sea-urchins, seals, and porpoises.

It is time to reset the clock from the rise and fall of the tide, to the come and go of the school bus. Pack your bag and put in a few treasures—some gull feathers, a few shells, a book of pressed leaves, a piece of quartz that came from a crack in the old rock on the point.

And, children, don't forget your toothbrushes.

Then "All aboard!" and around Deer Island, past Birch Island, past Pumpkin Island, and across Eggamoggin Reach, for the last time this year.

Take a farewell look at the waves and sky.
Take a farewell sniff of the salty sea.
A little bit sad
about the place you are leaving,
a little bit glad
about the place you are going.
It is a time of quiet wonder—for wondering, for instance: Where do hummingbirds go in a hurricane?

ONE MORNING
IN MAINE

1952

One morning in Maine, Sal woke up. She peeked over the top of the covers. The bright sunlight made her blink, so she pulled the covers up and was just about to go back to sleep when she remembered "today is the day I am going to Buck's Harbor with my father!"

Sal pushed back the covers, hopped out of bed, put on her robe and slippers, and hurried out into the hall.

There was little Jane, just coming out of her room. Sister Jane had wiggled out of her nightie, so Sal helped her put on her robe and slippers. "You don't want to catch cold and have to stay in bed, Jane, because this morning we are going to Buck's Harbor," Sal reminded her sister.

Together they went into the bathroom to get ready for breakfast. Sal squeezed out toothpaste on sister Jane's brush and said, "Be careful, Jane, and don't get it in your hair."

Then she squeezed some toothpaste on her own brush and when she started to brush her teeth something felt *very strange! One of her teeth felt loose!* She wiggled it with her tongue, then she wiggled it with her finger.

"Oh, dear!" thought Sal. "This *cannot* be true!"

Standing on the stool, she looked in the mirror and wiggled her tooth again. Sure enough, it was loose! You could even *see* it wiggle.

"Ma-a-a-ma!" she cried. "One of my teeth is loose! It will hurt and I'll have to stay in bed! I won't be able to eat my breakfast and go with Daddy to Buck's Harbor!" She came running down the stairs and into the kitchen.

"Why, Sal," said her mother, "that's nothing to worry about. That means that today you've become a big girl. Everybody's baby teeth get loose and come out when they grow up. A nice new bigger and better tooth will grow in when this one comes out."

"Did your baby teeth get loose and come out when you grew to be a big girl?" Sal asked her mother.

"Yes," she answered. "And then these nice large ones grew in. When Penny grew to be a big dog, his puppy teeth dropped out too."

"And will Jane's get loose too?" asked Sal.

"Yes," said her mother. "But not for a long time, not until she stops being a baby and grows up to be a big girl like you. Jane is so young that she hasn't even grown all her baby teeth yet. Now let's all go upstairs and brush our hair and get dressed for breakfast."

"It feels so different to be a big girl and have a loose tooth," said Sal, "especially when you are chewing. When is it going to come out?"

"Perhaps today, perhaps tomorrow," answered her mother. "But when your tooth does come out, you put it under your pillow and make a wish, and your wish is supposed to come true."

"I know what I'm going to wish for!" said Sal. "A nice cold choco—"

"But you mustn't tell anybody your wish, or it won't come true," cautioned her mother. "It's supposed to be a *secret* wish. Now finish your milk, Sal; then you can go out on the beach and help your father dig clams for lunch."

"I'm a big girl, and I can help him dig a lot of clams, fast," said Sal, "so we can hurry up and go to Buck's Harbor."

After breakfast, when Sal went out to help her father, she saw a fish hawk flying overhead, carrying a fish.

"I have a loose tooth!" Sal called up to the fish hawk. The fish hawk flew straight to her nest on top of a tree without answering. She was too busy feeding breakfast to her baby fish hawk.

Sal wondered for a moment if the baby fish hawk had any teeth to chew his breakfast. Then she started on down toward the beach where her father was digging clams.

When she came near to the water she saw a loon.

"I have a loose tooth!" Sal called to the loon. "And today I have started to be a big girl."

The loon didn't say anything but kept swimming in circles. Then he ducked his beak in the water and snapped out a herring. Then he swallowed it *whole*, without a single chew.

"Perhaps loons don't have teeth," thought Sal, and she was just turning to go on her way when a seal poked his head up out of the water.

"I have a loose tooth!" Sal said to the seal, and the seal, being just as curious as most seals, swam nearer to have a good look.

"See?" said Sal, and she walked closer, right down onto the slippery seaweeds at the water's edge.

The seal swam nearer, and Sal was stooping nearer when O-O-Oops! she slipped on the seaweed and fell kasploosh!

The seal disappeared beneath the water and the loon laughed, "Luh-hoo-hoo-hoo-hoo-hooh!"

Sal wasn't hurt a bit, so she laughed too, then she got up carefully and started on down the shore to help her father dig clams.

She paused to watch some sea gulls have breakfast. They were dropping mussels down on a rock to crack the mussel shells, just like nuts. Then they flew down to eat the insides.

"Do sea gulls have teeth?" wondered Sal as she wiggled her own loose one with her tongue. She thought of her secret wish and smiled, then hurried down the beach to where she could see her father.

"Daddy! I have a loose tooth!" she shouted. "And when it drops out I'm going to put it under my pillow and wish a wish. You can even see it wiggle!"

Her father stopped digging clams to watch while Sal wiggled her tooth for him. "You're growing into a big girl when you get a loose tooth!" he said. "What are you going to wish for when it drops out?"

"I can't tell you that," said Sal solemnly, "because it's supposed to be a *secret* wish."

"Oh, yes, so it is," her father agreed.

"May I help you dig clams?" Sal asked.

"I'm almost finished," he replied, "but you can help if you like. First, you must take off your shoes and socks, and roll up your pants too, so that they won't get all wet and muddy."

Sal took off her shoes and socks and put them on a dry rock. She rolled up her pants and waded into the muddy gravel to help her father. He dug in the mud with his clam rake, and then they looked carefully and felt around in the muddy hole for clams.

"I found a tiny baby one!" said Sal.

"You certainly did," said her father. "But it's too small. We just keep the large ones, like this. Let's put the baby clam back in the mud so he can grow to be a big clam some day."

"He *is* such a baby clam, and I guess he is too small," she agreed.

"I guess he isn't even big enough to have all his baby teeth," said Sal, placing the tiny clam tenderly back in the mud.

"Clams don't have teeth," grunted her father, digging another rakeful of mud.

"Not even big clams have teeth?" asked Sal.

"Not even big clams," her father assured her.

"Do baby fish hawks and big fish hawks have teeth?" asked Sal.

"No," said her father.

"Do loons have teeth?" she asked, "and gulls?"

"No."

"Do seals have teeth?"

"Yes, they have 'em," he answered.

"And do their teeth get loose like this?" asked Sal, opening her mouth to show her loose tooth.

"O-owh!" she said with great surprise. She felt with her tongue, and she felt with her muddy fingers.

"Why it's *gone!*" she said sadly, feeling once more just to make sure. The loose tooth was really and truly gone. The salty mud from her fingers tasted bitter, and she made a bitter-tasting face that was almost a face like crying.

"Did you swallow it, Sal?" her father asked with a concerned smile.

"No." She shook her head sadly. "I was too busy asking to do any swallowing. It just dropped itself out. It's gone, and I can't put it under my pillow and make my wish come true!"

"That's too bad," her father sympathized. "But you are growing into a big girl, and big girls don't cry about a little thing like that. They wait for another tooth to come loose and make a wish on that one."

"Maybe we can find my tooth where it dropped," said Sal, hopefully feeling around in the muddy gravel where the clams live.

Sal's father helped her look, but a muddy tooth looks so much like a muddy pebble, and a muddy pebble looks so much like a muddy tooth, that they hunted and hunted without finding it.

"We'll have to stop looking and take our clams back to the house, Sal," her father said at last, "or we won't have time for the trip to the village." He washed off the clams in the clean salt water of the bay, and Sal reluctantly stopped looking and waded in to wash the mud from her feet and hands.

"I guess some clam will find my tooth and get what I wished for," said Sal. "If we come back here tomorrow and find a clam eating a chocolate ice-cream cone, why, we'll have to take it away from him and make him give my tooth back too," she said.

While Sal put on her socks and shoes her father packed seaweed around the clams to keep them moist and fresh.

"Now, let's hurry back to the house," he said, "and in a few minutes we'll be on our way to Buck's Harbor in the boat to get milk and groceries."

"Okay," Sal answered, scrambling to her feet.

She gave one last look at the muddy place where she'd lost her tooth and then started walking back along the shore with her father. She walked along slowly, looking at her feet so that her father could not see her face, in case it looked almost like crying.

"Oh! See what I've found!" she exclaimed, stooping to pick up a feather.

"It's a gull's feather," said her father, pausing for Sal to pick it up.

"Did a gull lose it? Will another feather grow in where this one dropped out?" asked Sal.

"Yes, Sal, that's right," answered her father.

"Maybe sea gulls put dropped-out feathers under their pillows and wish secret wishes," Sal suggested.

"Sea gulls don't use pillows, but I suppose they can make wishes," her father said.

"Then I'll make my wish on this *feather*," Sal decided.

"Perhaps the sea gull has already made a wish on that feather and the wish is used up," suggested her father.

"Oh, no," Sal said definitely, "he didn't, you see. I guess because he was too busy flying and not looking back. He didn't notice it was loose when he brushed his feathers this morning, so he didn't expect it would drop out. He doesn't even know it's gone," she convinced herself. She closed her eyes tight and wished her secret wish.

When they reached home Sal's mother and sister Jane were waiting with a box of empty milk bottles to return to the store and a list of things to buy.

"I'll have a nice clam chowder ready for your lunch when you get back," said Sal's mother, waving good-by.

"I'll take good care of Jane," Sal promised. "I'm a big girl and I can watch so she doesn't tumble into the water."

Sal and Jane and their father went down to the shore and got aboard their boat.

Sal and Jane put on their life preservers while their father prepared to start the outboard motor. He pulled and he pulled on the rope to start it, but the outboard motor just coughed and sputtered and wouldn't start.

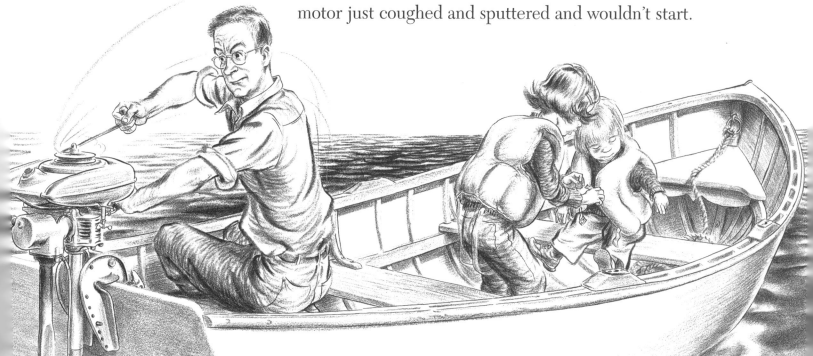

So he had to row the boat all the way across the bay to Buck's Harbor
where the store was.

The harbor was full of boats, and Sal's father rowed their boat among them, up to
a landing, and tied it so it would not drift away while they were at the store. They all
climbed ashore, and Sal's father brought along the milk bottles. He brought the
outboard motor too, so Mr. Condon who ran the garage could fix it.

As they came up the path to the village Mr. Condon was outside his garage,
putting gas into a car.

"I have a tooth out!" Sal greeted. "And our
outboard motor won't run."

"My, such trouble!" Mr. Condon commented, and after he had admired the empty place where Sal's tooth was missing they took the outboard motor into the garage to find why it wouldn't run. Mr. Condon pinched a little with his pliers, tunked a bit with his hammer, and then, after selecting a large wrench, he took out the spark plug.

"Came right out, just like that tooth of yours, didn't it, Sal?" he said, holding it up to the light. "Humph!" he grunted, tossing it on the floor. "Needs a new plug!"

Sal was just about to ask how long it would take for a new spark plug to grow in when Mr. Condon reached up on the shelf and picked out a brand new one, and put it in the motor.

Sal picked up the old spark plug and handed it to sister Jane. Jane was so little that she didn't understand about secret wishes. Jane was so little that she couldn't even say ice-cream cone! So Sal wished the secret wish for Jane on the spark plug.

Mr. Condon pulled the rope, and the motor started right up, just as good as new. Sal's father thanked him and picked up the motor and the milk bottles. Jane carried her spark plug, Sal carried her feather, and they said good-by and walked across the street to where Mr. Condon's brother kept store.

"Well, look who's here!" said the Mr. Condon who kept store.

"I have a tooth out!" Sal shouted, returning Mr. Condon's greeting.

She showed the empty place where her tooth had been, first to Mr. Condon, then to Mr. Ferd Clifford and Mr. Oscar Staples, who were sitting in the store talking about trapping lobster and how the fish were biting.

"Don't put your tongue in the empty place," Mr. Clifford advised, "and a nice shiny gold one like mine will grow in."

"But I didn't know soon enough," said Sal, looking confused.

"Hawh!" said Mr. Condon, chuckling. "Don't you go worryin' about everything these jokers suggest. I don't suppose," he added, opening up his freezer, "that you could eat an ice-cream cone with one of your teeth out?"

"Oh, yes, I could!" said Sal. "And it's supposed to be chocolate!"

"And this little lady?" he questioned, turning to Jane.

"Hers is supposed to be vanilla, so the drips won't spot, and you'd better push it together tight, so it won't drop off," Sal dictated, "because she's still almost a baby and doesn't even have all of her first teeth."

After Mr. Condon had put the groceries and milk in the box, they thanked him
once more and waved good-by. They walked down the path to the harbor and down
the runway to the float where their boat was tied. They all climbed aboard, carrying
the outboard motor, the box of milk and groceries, the feather, the spark plug, and
the ice-cream cones.

While their father fastened the outboard motor to the boat Sal and Jane finished
their ice-cream cones.

"I want s'more!" Jane demanded.

"Silly!" exclaimed Sal. "Our wishes are all used up." Then she remembered that
she was growing up, and just like a grownup she said, "Besides, Jane, two ice-cream
cones would ruin your appetite. When we get home we're going to have

CLAM CHOWDER FOR LUNCH!"

ABOUT ROBERT McCLOSKEY

Robert McCloskey wrote and illustrated just eight books during his distinguished career, but those extraordinary, timeless books forever changed the world of children's literature. From a determined family of mallard ducks to the enterprising young Homer Price with his uncle's doughnut machine, McCloskey created some of the most memorable characters and images in twentieth-century children's books. He has been recognized time and again for his impact on literature, both for his own books and for his illustrations in books by other authors. He received two Caldecott Medals and three Caldecott Honors. In 2000, the Library of Congress named him a Living Legend. Statues commemorate his work, and his devoted fan base crosses generations.

Robert McCloskey, or Bob, as he was always called, was born on September 15, 1914. He grew up in Hamilton, Ohio, with his two younger sisters, Dorothy and Melba, playing Kick the Can in the streets with his pals. Everyone in his family had chores—Bob's was to haul the family's ice for the week in his red wagon.

Bob attended public school. At an early age he became interested in art, music, and inventing mechanical devices—all hobbies that eventually found their way into his books. His uncle John taught him to play the piano, but Bob hated the lessons. He loved music, though, and taught himself to play the harmonica. Once he was even invited to play the harmonica in a band on a local radio show. Bob put his love of tinkering and inventing to work around the house, often with mixed results. A taffy maker he created for his mother was unreliable and tended to splatter the kitchen walls. But his parents thought his mechanical abilities were good enough that he should pursue a career in car repair.

His parents did not believe art was a reliable way to make a living. Drawing became Bob's focus, though, and in 1932 he won a scholarship to the Vesper George Art School in Boston. Just two years later he received his first important commission—he created bas-reliefs for the municipal building in his

Left: Robert McCloskey with his Meccano Set, circa 1925; top: as a toddler; bottom: playing the harmonica, circa 1940.

hometown. The following autumn he moved to New York to study at the National Academy of Design, where he exhibited his work and won the President's Award. He spent two summers painting on Cape Cod, but sold only a few watercolors while there.

Realizing he wouldn't be able to support himself on fine art alone, he went to visit legendary children's book editor May Massee at Viking Junior Books in New York. "I came into her office with my folio under my arm and sat on the edge of my chair," he remembered. "She looked at the examples of 'great art' that I had brought along (they were woodcuts, fraught with black drama). I don't remember just the words she used to tell me to get wise to myself and to shelve the dragons, Pegasus, and limpid pool business and learn how and what to 'art' with. I think we talked mostly of Ohio."

Bob soon moved back to Ohio and began to draw and paint the things around him. The result was *Lentil* (1940), a semi-autobiographical story about a boy and his harmonica in a typical Midwestern town. Soon after the book's publication, Bob moved back to Boston. It was while living there that he got the

Pencil sketches from letters to May Massee.

idea for his most famous book, *Make Way for Ducklings*. He wrote, "I had first noticed the ducks when walking through the Boston Public Garden every morning on my way to art school. When I returned to Boston four years later, I noticed the traffic problem of the ducks and heard a few stories about them. The book just sort of developed from there."

Make Way for Ducklings was published in 1941 and received the 1942 Caldecott Medal, the most prestigious prize in picture book illustration. The beloved Mallard family has become a mainstay in libraries and picture book collections, and was immortalized in bronze statues by sculptor Nancy Schon. One set of the sculptures can be found in the Boston Public Garden in Boston, Massachusetts, and the other is in Novodevichy Park, Moscow, Russia. In 2003, *Make Way for Ducklings* was named the official state book of Massachusetts.

Homer Price, Bob's first chapter book, was published in 1943. A few years earlier the United States had entered World War II. Bob was sent to Fort McClellan, Alabama, where, as a sergeant, he was put to work drawing visual aids

Top: studies of ducks; bottom: sculptor Nancy Schon's Mallard family sculpture in Boston, Massachusetts.

Top: Peggy McCloskey, 1952; bottom: using his daughters as models, 1958.

for the army. He said, "They were never quite sure what to do with me. As an artist, I did not exactly fit in."

During the war, Bob married Peggy Durand, the daughter of renowned author Ruth Sawyer with whom he later collaborated on the book *Journey Cake Ho!* (a Caldecott Honor Book). In 1945, the couple had their first child, Sally. When Sal was one year old, the McCloskeys moved to Maine and bought an island that would become the center of the universe for Bob and his growing family. Just like the father duck in *Make Way for Ducklings*, Bob had found a safe place on an island to raise his family.

Blueberries for Sal (a Caldecott Honor Book) was written and illustrated in Bob's island studio while the McCloskeys awaited the arrival of their second child. The book was meant as a distraction for the real Sal, who was upset that she would no longer be the only child. To her surprise (and, later, embarrassment), the charmingly improbable story about a mix-up with a couple of bears made her very much the center of attention and immortalized her, as well as her mother.

Bob had been awarded the Prix de Rome for painting in 1939, but was not allowed to travel abroad during the war. In 1948, just after their second daughter Jane's birth, the McCloskey family went to Italy where they lived for one year while Bob studied at the American Academy in Rome.

The McCloskeys' return to their island life in 1949 inspired Bob to create more books about his family and Maine: *One Morning in Maine* (a Caldecott Honor Book); *Burt Dow, Deep-Water Man*; and *Time of Wonder*. *Time of Wonder*, which was written for his daughter Jane, was awarded the 1958 Caldecott Medal, making Robert McCloskey the first artist to receive the award twice.

In the 1960s, Bob illustrated Keith Robertson's *Henry Reed* books. After that he spent his time painting in his studio and designing puppets. His puppets were marvels of anatomically correct movement, each made from hundreds of tiny pieces crafted on his lathe in his studio and assembled like an old-fashioned watch. He tinkered happily with the inner workings of a mole, mouse, and pigeon puppet, and he molded incredibly expressive faces for them—they could lift eyebrows or look as though they had just sucked on a lemon. Sadly, he never developed the puppets for public presentation. He abandoned the project, concluding that his work had been preempted by the new graphics of computer technology. It was a new way of thinking about art that he struggled with in his later years, but never entirely grasped.

Bob's wife Peggy was the practical one in the family—paying bills, keeping financial records, and responding to fan mail. She was a librarian for some years, and an excellent cook, and had a gift for hospitality. Sometimes her love of people was hard on her husband, who needed solitude; and his need for quiet was hard on her in return. Still their strengths worked together. Peggy died in 1990.

Few people ever knew that Bob was a painter in addition to being an illustrator. Always the perfectionist, he never showed or sold his works after he began his career in children's books. Some of his paintings are unfinished, but many that he did complete are exceptionally beautiful. As an illustrator he was recognized as a fine draftsman. His paintings are just as carefully executed, but by contrast they are flat, patterned, and semi-abstract, reflecting his experimentation with concepts of dynamic symmetry and balance borrowed

Top: with one of his puppets; bottom: with his daughters and pet English setter, Penny, on the porch of May Massee's house in Croton Falls, New York, circa 1953.

ДОРОГУ УТЯТАМ

Роберт Макклоски

Above: Russian edition of *Make Way for Ducklings*; below: with Barbara Bush, following their trip to Moscow, Russia, in 1991; bottom: after receiving the Living Legend medal from the Library of Congress in 2000.

from classic art forms. Much of his work consists of portraits of Sal, Jane, and Peggy. He found a wealth of subject matter in Mexico and in St. Thomas in the Virgin Islands where the McCloskeys also lived, but he always went back to painting the world of his beloved island home in Maine.

The author who once declared, "It is just sort of an accident that I write books. I really think up stories in pictures and just fill in between the pictures with a sentence or a paragraph or a few pages of words," was recognized with countless honors and awards throughout his life.

In 1991 Bob traveled to Russia with President and Mrs. George H. W. Bush to present a set of duckling statues from the children of the United States to the children of Russia. In 1992, at the American Library Association's annual Newbery–Caldecott banquet, librarians gave him a standing ovation as he was presented with a special citation celebrating the fiftieth anniversary of *Make Way for Ducklings*. In 2000, he was named a Living Legend by the Library of Congress. Bob held a special place in the hearts of teachers, librarians, and booksellers, and his rare appearances were invariably standing-room-only events. But he was a shy man, and preferred being at his quiet home in Maine to almost anything else. He died in 2003 after a brief illness.

Each one of Robert McCloskey's legendary eight books is still in print today, and they continue to entertain, reassure, and surprise readers as they have for more than sixty years.